Sotherton Abbey

Jane Austen Meets Santa Fe

Published by Ashley House
614 47th St.
Los Alamos, New Mexico

ISBN: 978-0-9664337-4-6

Library of Congress Control Number: 2009913402

Printed in Canada

Sotherton Abbey
Jane Austen Meets Santa Fe

By Inez Ross

Ashley House

Books by Inez Ross

The Strange Disappearance of Uncle Dudley:
A Child's Story of Los Alamos

The Bear and The Castle:
The James Oliver Curwood Story

The Adobe Castle:
A Southwest Gothic Romance

Without a Wagon:
Hiking Into History

Perilous Pursuit on the Santa Fe Trail

Persuaded:
A Great Lakes Story

Tales From a Teacher:
As Told By Lucille McCleskey

For Whitney Marie Ross

Jane Austen wrote the story of Catherine Morland, who left her country home to visit the popular resort town of Bath in the England of the Eighteenth Century. The book is *Northanger Abbey*.

Inspired by Jane Austen's book, this author is telling the story of Christina Dashwood, who leaves her country home in the American Midwest to visit Santa Fe, the popular cultural center of the Southwest, in the Twentieth Century.

The Author wishes to thank Jane Austen for continuing to entertain readers in the Twenty-first Century. We enjoy the films, Broadway shows, sequels, and spinoffs based on her works. The yearly meeting of JASNA, Jane Austen Society of North America, gives us opportunity to discuss her characters and plots, and learn more about life in the Regency Era.

Other thanks for help on this book go to my friends and editors: D'Anne Andrykovich for the cover art, Phyllis Morgan for her careful editing, Jennifer Reglien for her commentary and horse savvy, Dexter Sutherland for crucial tweaks, Anita Quintana for the digital design, and my sister Lois Whalen for being my favorite critic.

Chapter I

*No one would have supposed her
born to be an heroine.*

—JANE AUSTEN

Christina Dashwood had always seen herself
as an heroine.

She was only average in appearance, short
and rather bony, but began to fill out pleasingly
as she approached adolescence. Her long hair
was an ordinary brown, but waved nicely. The
only flaw an attentive observer might detect was
a chipped front tooth, incurred as she had leaned
over the seat of the school bus when it lurched
during one of her story telling sessions for the
smaller children.

Living in the relative seclusion of a small farm with her younger sister and her parents just before the incursion of that electronic marvel that sends pictures of heroines into our living rooms, she was more interested in reading and in the occasional film offered at the cinema in the nearby village. Consequently, her heroine models were shaped by a series of movie stars and literary characters as she grew up.

When she was driving the family cow home to the barn for evening milking, she carried a long stick as a rifle and threatened to kill the lurking rustlers she saw behind the bushes.

When she lined up the chairs in the dining room to simulate the cabin of an airplane, she caused her little sister Lilly to be a stewardess serving tea to the teddy bear passengers, while she sat in the large arm chair at the front of the plane, piloting the aircraft through the worst storms in the history of aviation.

In junior high she became a princess. She and her classmates formed a Medieval group in the Kingdom of Atenveldt at the edge of the Knowne Worlde. Her own gown and headdress gave her a superior status and she began to talk forsoothly and seek advancement as Aleta of Alnilam. But her hopes were dashed when the College of Heralds would not accept her name and coat of arms. "You cannot be from a star, and the canine on your device looks more like Snoopy than an heraldic beast." (Alnilam is the middle star in the belt of the constellation Orion: her choice of canine was a beagle.) The national medieval organization, although admittedly playing at history, kept strict requirements for potential membership.

In high school she became entranced by her English teacher who had dark hair and green eyes. She pictured her as a Southern belle from *Gone with the Wind*. Miss Johnson was known secretly by Christina and her friends as Scarlett O'Johnson and became the subject of their whispered comments on her hairdo and daily wardrobe choices. Their favorite was her green woolen suit with the flared skirt.

During her senior year she fell in love with her history teacher. Mr. Saxon was a retired college professor who had been persuaded by his friend, the school principal, to return to the classroom to replace a teacher who had resigned. Mr. Saxon had iron gray curly hair, a thin mustache, and a silver topped cane. The students imagined that his slight limp was due to a war wound incurred while saving his comrades in terrible combat. But Jerry Smith, who sat at the desk behind her, whispered that the injury was probably due to a

broken leg incurred when his wife pushed him
off the back porch. Christina and her Blue Stock-
ing friends dismissed that notion as a scurrilous
rumor.

The charm of Mr. Saxon with his elderly mien,
courtly manners, and British accent caused his
mere suggestions for extra reading to be taken
more seriously than were the textbook requirements. Mr. Saxon was fond of 18th Century English literature, and Christina was soon reading
Johnson and Pope and absorbing the cadences
of stately prose and pithy poetry.

But her own Enlightenment came one day
during the era of the Napoleonic Wars, when Mr.
Saxon casually mentioned the connection of that
era with his most admired novelist, relatively unknown during her own day, and now the focus of
increasing popularity. Her name was Jane Austen, and her novel *Pride and Prejudice* would
be required reading for their freshman year in
college.

Christina immediately found the novel in the
library and proceeded to read everything else
she could find by or about Jane Austen. Thus
her 18th Century gave way to the Regency Era,
and the tiara and tabard, which had already been
dropped with the demise of the Medieval Maid-

ens, gave way to empire waistlines, pelisses, and spencer jackets.

In this progression of romantic interests our heroine must, of course, at some point encounter a hero. The event which brought that about, along with the challenge which changed her life, came during her senior year. It was a call which led her out of her ordinary world into a world of exotic adventure. It came on one Monday morning when Mr. Saxon made the announcement of a contest which would award the winner with a trip to Sotherton Abbey.

Chapter II

*If adventures will not befall a
young lady in her own village, she
must seek them abroad.*

—JANE AUSTEN

"What is this 'Search for Sotherton Abbey'?
Was she lost?"

"No, Daddy. That's not a person. It's the name
of the seminar. It's a six week course in Regency."

"Where is Regency? Is it north of Detroit?"

"Daddy. Stop teasing! Regency is a time period
in English history. The seminar will be in Santa
Fe. Mary Sidney is going. It'll be such fun. Look
at this brochure."

Mr. Dashwood laid aside his pipe, took the
little pamphlet, and settled back to browse for
more objections to this costly project. "It says

here that transportation to the college will be at your own expense."

"I'm under eighteen. Can't I still go there by train and use our family railroad pass?" Christina was ready to counter all objections to her dream.

Mr. Dashwood had worked for the Michigan Railway as telegraph operator and ticket agent for many years. Settling his family in Tondaga, Michigan, he had bought forty acres of bargain land and a book titled *Thirty Acres and Independence.* But after ten years of trying to harvest enough corn and hay for his three cows from the stubborn ground, he decided that the book had been written by a retired gentleman with three strapping sons and a Herculean wife, all living on a tract of level black loam, not for a railroad worker with a family consisting of a delicate wife with two school-age daughters, who lived on dry clay hills that seemed to get the least rainfall in all of Shiawassee County.

"We've been saving for your tuition at Livingston College, Tina. This seminar seems pretty expensive for six weeks out west."

"But it will give me two college credits, and I'm sure the credits will transfer to Livingston."

Mr. Dashwood frowned. "Credit for credit, Livingston will be much less expensive, my Dear."

Then Tina submitted her final card. "Mr. Saxon says there's an essay contest based on Jane Austen. The prize is free tuition for the seminar. I've read all six of Jane Austen's novels, and Miss Johnson says I'm a good writer. I'm sure I can win, Daddy. Let me apply."

"Very well. If you can win the tuition and your mother and sister can do without you for a few weeks, you have my blessing."

Mrs. Dashwood was hesitant. She had once been frightened by a man with very dark skin and a black mustache. He had come asking for work when she was alone in the house. "Those Mexican people don't speak English," she said. "I could hardly understand him."

Christina put her arm around her mother and spoke in a most dulcet tone of voice. "Mamma, this will be in NEW Mexico, a state of the United States. Santa Fe is the capital. The seminar is all in English with professors visiting from every-where in the nation."

Younger sister Lilly had mixed emotions about Christina's proposed trip. The jealousy of being unable to partake in the glorious adventure her-self was balanced by the thought that she could have their shared bedroom all to herself, and she was mentally already taking down Christina's posters of Cornel Wilde and Lawrence Olivier and expanding the space for her Roy Rogers and Gene Autry photos. "How long, when you get back, will it be before you leave for college?" she asked.

Christina, in her expansive optimism, generously assured her sister she could have most of the dresser space and all of the wall space for herself, and added, "Just leave two drawers for me for when I come home for Christmas." And all aglow with happiness, she sat down to begin writing.

Chapter III

*What have wealth or grandeur to
do with happiness? Grandeur has
but little...but wealth has much.*

—JANE AUSTEN

It is often the case that a social group has one member whose talents and privilege are so much greater than that of the others that that person is either envied with scorn or looked up to with great admiration. For Mary Sidney, in Christina's class, it was the latter. In every school theatrical Mary was either the star or the director. In elections for cheerleader or class president the winner was Mary Sidney. Her parents owned an electric motor factory in Tondaga, and her stylish wardrobe was evidence of a large clothing allowance. But her warm personality and generous attitude continually expanded her circle of friends. Mary Sidney was looked up to and admired.

Christina was surprised that Mary was entering the writing competition for the Santa Fe Regency seminar. "Aren't your folks giving you the trip and tuition?" she asked. "Why do you need to write a contest entry?"

"Oh, Tina, I'm sure you'll win over me," she replied. "You've read all the Austen books, and I've read only one. But even if I get a low score, the fact that I entered will look good on my college application. My father wants me to attend Harvard, and the more high school activities I can list, the better my chances will be for admission."

For the first time Christina's admiration for Mary was tainted with envy and a feeling of injustice. Mary would easily add another prize to her already lengthy list of honors. A win for Mary would be just another feather in her cap, but it would be the end to Christina's summer dream. She felt as if a door were already slamming shut in her face.

Lilly was encouraging. "You'll win, Tina," she said. "You can write about all of the books."

But Christina remembered Miss Johnson's saying that a good essay has just one focus. How could she display her extensive reading and have just one thesis point? After long deliberation, she came up with the brilliant idea of describing all the heroes, but showing which one would be the ideal suitor.

With a short deadline and a stout heart she began to work.

But the research for her topic required looking into all of the novels again, and the search became a task more onerous than anticipated.

Then, as she began to type on the old Royal typewriter that her father had brought home from his ticket office, its keys kept jamming and locking together. When she finally accepted that she must proceed more slowly, the spool ran out of ribbon and would not reverse.

She was forced to start over and copy the entire essay in longhand. This process was even slower because, though she was a quick note taker, her penmanship was legible only with a slow and deliberate pace. She sat writing at the kitchen table. The household was quiet. The clock in the hallway struck midnight. Her eyes and her hand ached. Mouser, the gray cat, jumped up on the table and wanted to play with the moving pen. Pushing the cat aside, she laid her head on the table to take a brief rest before continuing.

Ten gentlemen stood before her. The tallest was Mr. Darcy from *Pride and Prejudice.* "I am very wealthy," he said. "If you marry me you will be mistress of Pemberley which has a library that is the work of many generations."

"But you are too proud," she told him. "You look down on my family because my father is a common laborer."

Next to him stood Colonel Brandon from *Sense and Sensibility*. He put his hand on her arm and drew her close until her head was against his chest. "Marry me," he said, "and I will take care of you forever."

"But you are too old for me," she replied. "You wear a flannel waistcoat." She could feel its softness against her cheek. It felt more like fur than flannel and she awoke with a start. Daylight was showing through the kitchen window and she could hear her mother coming down the stairs. The fuzzy flannel dissolved, becoming Mouser's angora fur, and her dream evaporated in the panic of her unfinished task.

She was forced to finish writing on the school bus, which jostled on the gravel roads, and the quality of her penmanship suffered in inverse proportion to the speed of the bus and her nervous haste.

The bell rang, and students came forward to submit their work in the English classroom. A quick look at her essay brought another stab of panic. On the third page was a large oily paw print! Mouser had sampled the butter on the kitchen table and left her mark on the paper.

Her request for an extension so that she might rewrite was declined with a smile from Miss Johnson. "Superintendent Shufelter is coming right away to collect all the entries. Handwritten essays are fine, and yours looks very neat," she said, glancing at the first page.

Her despair was deepened when she saw Mary Sidney deposit her neatly typed essay on the top of the pile.

Christina's exhaustion and disappointment would last forever, she thought, and she knew she would die before the end of the week when results of the competition would be announced.

Chapter IV

*...all the anxiety of expectation
and the pain of disappointment.*

—JANE AUSTEN

A true heroine has a noble demeanor and carries on bravely and cheerfully in spite of difficulties. Christina determined to maintain a façade of equanimity in spite of her failure to produce a polished essay for the competition. She remembered what her drama teacher Mr. Ramsey had taught her in acting class. When everyone was terrified of appearing on stage for the first time in front of a large audience, he lectured them on his Position Theory, which was summed up in the order "Assume the Bodily Position." That meant one should envisage what a poised and professional actor would look like and then assume that physical stance. If the body appeared relaxed, the actual feeling would follow.

So she held her head high, smiled at everyone, and acted as if the whole essay episode was an inconsequential event of the past. Her acting succeeded until she went home where depression and tears threatened to engulf her. At school she maintained her stance and actually began to feel heroic, until a week later when the announcement was read in the morning homeroom bulletin: "Congratulations to Mary Sidney for writing the winning essay in the Austen Regency Tuition contest."

Christina immediately walked over to Mary with a smile and gave her a congratulatory hug. But then, her acting was carried too far because when Mary thanked her and added, "But you'll still be attending the seminar also won't you?" Christina replied, "Oh sure, I've sent in my application."

Immediately she berated herself for telling the lie, which would eventually have to result in an embarrassing explanation of the truth.

Determination and the resilience of youth revived her spirits and she felt that all may not be lost. There could be perhaps another way to obtain her trip. Perhaps her parents would relent and give permission after all. She wondered if her father's stipulation would hold when he knew how disappointed she was. Surely the family finances could be stretched somehow to cover her tuition.

The Dashwood farmhouse was a two-story edifice with three bedrooms on the upper level, one of which was a spare room used for storage. The stovepipe from the living room coal stove went through it on the way to the roof and furnished heat for the upstairs. Around the pipe was a circular vent in the floor of the spare room, which not only let the heat rise, but also made any conversation from the living room audible from above.

That night after turning restlessly in her bed for what she thought were hours, she arose quietly so as not to awake Lilly and crept into the spare room where she lay down on the floor with her ear near the stovepipe vent. Her mother and father were involved in conversation below.

"Tina seemed a little glum at supper tonight," Mr. Dashwood observed.

"Yes, even Lilly was out of spirits. She feels sad that Tina won't be taking the trip." Christina was encouraged to hear her mother's sympathy.

"Maybe after we send the calves to veal market, we can look at the bank balance again." Mr.

Dashwood was weakening and Christina crossed her fingers.

"But I really think it's for the best that she be here this summer, John. We really need both girls when haying is on. The trip to Lansing to buy college clothes will be next. And Mrs. Fedorski was telling me how expensive the college books are. She said Frankie paid forty-nine dollars for one psychology book last year!"

"Yes, I guess we'd better hold to the original agreement. Youth is fraught with many disappointments, and Tina will get over this one. There will be other summer trips, and in the meantime she'll be looking forward to Livingston. Is there any coffee left in the pot, Laura?"

The conversation ended with the sound of cups on saucers and Christina had to roll over from her eavesdropping position lest her tears run down the stovepipe.

Chapter V

A loss may be sometimes a gain.

–JANE AUSTEN

The following morning the school secretary brought a note to the homeroom teacher, and all heads turned as she thanked the secretary, handed the note to Christina and said, "Mr. Shufelter wants to see you, Christina."

This was definitely a time to practice the Assume-the-Bodily-Position Theory. Christina walked out with her head held high while all eyes and whispered questions followed her.

Mr. Shufelter was a broad-shouldered gray-haired man with bulldog jowls and a matching voice. His mere presence in the halls could subdue any noise and correct student deportment.

He sat behind his desk with his usual frown, but his words did not match his facial expression. "We have good news, Christina, about this recent essay contest. Genesee County did not send any entries, and the contest board was informed that the prize money had to be awarded or forfeited. The judges then reviewed all the entries, and decided, that on the whole, the Washtenaw entries were inferior to all of ours. They ruled that our second-place entry be awarded the tuition scholarship. And that entry is yours."

Stunned and shocked, Christina was slow to understand and to realize her good fortune. "What?" she stammered.

"Here is the commentary from the panel. 'Although lacking focus and technical perfection, this essay is superior in its enthusiasm, humor, and natural writing style. It is our unanimous opinion that it clearly earns the extra prize.' So, congratulations, Christina."

She was sure her feet did not touch the floor on her way to class, nor all that day. Celestial music continually rang in her ears. And what a flurry at home! Her parents smiled, Lilly danced wildly with her arms in the air, and Mouser ran in fright to hide under the davenport.

The semester dragged to an end. Applications were filled and sent, graduation was formalized, new clothes were bought, train tickets purchased, and borrowed suitcases sat open on the floor to receive the final items for travel to New Mexico.

"Will Mary Sidney be traveling with you?" Mr. Dashwood hung up the phone, and turned to Christina with the question.

"No, she's flying. Her folks are taking her to Lansing to catch the plane. Maybe I can ride with them to get the train there."

"The problem is, I just learned that the Bluewater now does not connect with the Chicago-New Mexico train. That means a bus to Battle Creek to get the Southern Michigan train to Chicago."

Mr. Dashwood frowned and Mrs. Dashwood broke in with her reaction. "I don't like the idea of her having to go on the bus by herself with all that luggage. John, why don't you drive her to Battle Creek? I would go with you, but Saturday is the day I'm to have my Women's Club meeting here. I'm overdue for my turn to be hostess and really can't put it off."

The morning of departure was sunny and warm. Lilly was singing "Gonna Take a Sentimental Journey" in a loud voice, and her mother was packing cheese sandwiches with Women's Club cookies in a large sack. "I hope you have a seat to yourself for overnight on the train," she said. "Don't sit all night with a strange man. Be sure to call us as soon as you arrive in Santa Fe." She had tears in her eyes as she handed Christina the lunch sack.

Hugs and kisses preceded the last goodbyes. Her father loaded her luggage and drove Christina off toward her exotic destination.

Chapter VI

There isn't a train I wouldn't take,
No matter where it's going.

—EDNA ST. VINCENT MILLAY

After checking her bag, Christina and her father were emerging from the baggage room of the little depot at Battle Creek, when she spied a familiar figure entering the waiting room. "Mr. Saxon! Are you going by train? I thought you'd be taking the plane."

"Yes, Christina. I always prefer the train. We won't be in the same coach on the western train, but we'll be traveling together as far as Chicago, I guess."

"Oh, that's good! I'd like you to meet my father. Daddy, this is Mr. Saxon, my history professor for the seminar."

"How do you do, Professor Saxon," he replied extending his hand. "I'm John Dashwood, Tina's father."

"Not Professor, just teacher. I didn't quite attain professor status before I left for the army. Tina tells me you're an official of the railroad."

"Not official, just an agent at Tondaga, and a part-time farmer."

"Both important professions, nevertheless. As long as we have some time before the train arrives, I suggest we take some refreshment together in the little café across the way."

Tina was uneasy about having her father meet Mr. Saxon.

John Dashwood lacked a complete high school education, having left school early to find work to support his widowed mother and his sisters. But he had always been a great reader and considered himself a self-educated man. His lack of schooling was evident only if using words in conversation, which he had never himself heard pronounced. Christina recalled one occasion when he had referred to the Greek philosophers as "Platt-o and Sew-crates."

But over coffee and rolls in the Rail Café, the conversation remained light, and the two men warmed to each other in a very friendly manner. As they talked, she noticed the contrast between the reddened complexion and sandy hair of her father to that of Mr. Saxon's pale complexion and silvery mane. Her father's hands were calloused with large knuckles, and he wore no rings. Mr. Saxon's hands were slender and artistic. He wore a thin gold ring with scalloped edges on the little finger of his right hand, and the little finger on his left hand was curiously bent, but there were no other signs of age or hard labor.

The conversation had returned to the topic of agriculture and its advancing dominance by the larger landholders. Mr. Saxon expressed regret that the increasing importance of agriculture had not raised the social status or the profits of the farmer in direct proportion.

"Yes, the farmers in the eighteenth century were the landed gentry," remarked Mr. Dashwood. "It was an agrarian society, and agricultural concerns took precedence in those days. I recall that Mrs. Bennet said the horses could not be spared from the farm, even though going to Netherfield by carriage would have been more proper for Jane or Elizabeth."

Mr. Saxon laughed. "Yes, *Pride and Prejudice*! You are familiar with our favorite author, I see."

Christina was surprised. Her father had actually read *Pride and Prejudice*! And she was pleased that his comments had placed him in a favorable light with her erudite teacher.

The conversation was ended with the announcement from the stationmaster, "Wolverine! Chicago and points between: Kalamazoo, Dowagiac, Niles, Hammond, and Michigan City. Stay behind the yellow line until ready to board."

Christina's father gave her a hug and slipped a little folded packet of bills into her hand. "For extra spending money," he said.

Mr. Saxon helped her up the steps into the Chicago coach, and finding a seat by a window on the station side of the car, they waved goodbye as the train moved away.

Union Station at Chicago was filled with crowds of travelers to distant cities, as well as commuters headed for local trains and buses. Mr. Saxon showed her the Great Hall with its high ceiling and classic décor and led her to a special waiting room for first-class passengers. They did not have long to wait before the announcement came for their train, the Chicago-Los Angeles Chief, which they would ride as far as Lamy, New Mexico.

Although Tina's father was a railroad man, and the family had access to a railroad pass, they had never traveled far from home. She remembered going to Muskegon on the Grand Trunk as a small child, but longer trips on trains with dining facilities and sleeping cars were unknown to her. Although Mr. Saxon would be in a roomette in the first-class car, he explained that he would make a dinner reservation for both of them and come to her coach seat for her when it was time to accompany her to the diner.

"Till seven o'clock, then," he said, and left to go to his room.

She had brought along *Mansfield Park* to re-read and examine the passages about Sotherton, the large estate which was the focus of a special visit for the main characters. She had not remembered mention of an abbey in that book, and concluded that the name Sotherton Abbey had been chosen as title of the seminar because it was to focus on two of Jane Austen's books, *Mansfield Park* and *Northanger Abbey*. But the excitement of finally being on the train to New Mexico, and the attractions of the scenery along the way precluded any reading, and she sat in a daze as the countryside melted away behind the speeding train. The daze became a drowsy state. She leaned into the corner by the window and fell asleep.

She awoke with a start. A tall man in a business suit standing beside her was noisily trying to stow a large bag in the overhead shelf. The train was not moving. "Where are we?" she asked.

"Galesburg," he answered. "There may be a delay. I see an ambulance out there at the station. Must be someone got sick on the train."

She turned to see a gurney being lifted into the ambulance, doors closing, and a uniformed train attendant walking back toward the front of the train. A minute later the train began moving again. She looked at her watch, which read a little after six p.m.

The tall man sat down beside her, opened a newspaper, and settled himself to read, first adding, "The conductor will be coming for my ticket. Maybe he'll give us some information about the ambulance. Have you traveled this route before? We'll be crossing the Mississippi in awhile. It's always an interesting sight."

When asked, the conductor who took his ticket said, "I believe someone fell getting off the train in Galesburg. Passed out. I think she's revived. Ambulance came in a good hurry."

The Mississippi crossing was impressive. Three large barges, headed downriver, were passing beneath the train bridge. On the opposite shore the train entered Iowa at the town of Fort Madison. Christina looked out the window on the other side to see an old fort and a large riverboat anchored at the pier. She began to feel hungry, and looked at her sandwich sack, but remembering that Mr. Saxon would be taking her to the diner at seven, she put it aside and opened her book. Finally a voice on the loud speaker said, "All persons holding seven o'clock dinner reservations should proceed to the dining car. Please wait to be seated."

Seven fifteen, and still no Mr. Saxon. Could he have forgotten her? She decided to walk toward the front of the train. Perhaps she would meet him on the way. Passing through the lounge car, she noticed a sign directing her to a downstairs lunch counter and descending the little stairway, she inquired of the snack bar attendant. He could give her no information.

Forward again to the dining car, where she asked the waiter there, but he could give her no information. A managerial looking woman in blue uniform came forward and said, "We had a seven o'clock reservation for two who did not come. Maybe he fell asleep."

Now she was really concerned. Mr. Saxon would not oversleep his supper by an hour! She brushed past the waiter and the manager, then rushed forward to the sleeper car, bracing on the walls of the passageway and the closed doorways as the train jostled her, and ignoring the sign which said "Sleeping Car Passengers Only Beyond This Point." Around corners and into the second first-class car, she finally saw an attendant wearing a name tag on her white blouse, and stammered, "Miss Wolf, can you help me please? I'm looking for Mr. Saxon. Is he in this car?"

"I believe he was the man in Number 13, who became ill and had to get off at Galesburg." And noticing Christina's distress, she put an arm around her shoulder and gently inquired if she had been traveling with him, led Christina to a nearby seat, and comforted her with encouraging words.

Chapter VII

Worry is interest paid on trouble
before it falls due.

—DEAN WILLIAM RALPH INGE

Her stunned reaction had made her words almost unintelligible, but she managed to explain the situation and express her distress.

Miss Wolf attempted to calm her and explained that she could call home when they reached Kansas City. The train was scheduled for a longer stop there, giving her time to use a phone in the station. "I'm Nancy. Let me know if I can help you any more."

Christina returned to her seat in the coach-class car and tried to remain calm. There was no one to share her distress. Her seatmate had left to get coffee in the lounge car, but returned and began taking down his luggage from the overhead shelf as the train slowed to a stop at La Plata, where he got off. As the train began to move again, the conductor came along and asked, "Miss Dashwood? I have a message for you, a telegram that was received at La Plata."

With trembling hands she took it and read: MY HEALTH REQUIRES RETURN TO MICHIGAN FOR NOW. DO NOT WORRY. WILL CONTACT YOU IN SANTA FE. REGARDS, W. SAXON

At least he is alive, she sighed, and settled back to wait for the stop in Kansas City.

The station was crowded, and there was a line of people in front of the row of phone booths. When she finally entered one, she had difficulty getting a connection, lacked the proper change requested by the operator, and finally, worried that the train was about to depart, left without completing her call.

When she returned to her seat on the train, she found the companion seat occupied by a lady wearing a green feathered hat and a disappointed look. "Oh, are you sitting here? There don't seem to be any other seats. But I guess you're small enough. We can fit in, can't we?"

Christina had her doubts because the woman was of such ponderous bulk that she took up

more than her share of space, but she rose to let
Christina slide into the window seat. After a brief
exchange of amenities regarding where each was
from and what their destinations were, silence
ensued because the coach lights had been turned
off and most of their fellow travelers were settled
to sleep. Christina felt wide awake, still recovering from her recent shock and still worried, but
the green-hat lady fell into slumber almost immediately and began to snore with a soft whis-
tling sound, at the same time slumping to the
side, one fat arm resting against Christina. Christina pushed back gently, and the woman roused,
apologized, and shortly fell asleep again, this time
sagging heavily toward Christina with her whole
torso.

Christina recalled seeing vacant seats in the
lounge car and decided that sitting up all night
there might be better than being pressed against
this fleshy stranger, so she pushed the woman
upright, apologized, and stepping out into the
aisle, headed toward the lounge car. On her way
she saw passengers sprawled in various pos-
tures of sleep, some with blankets, some with
feet protruding into the aisle, some with their
own huge pillows to augment the tiny ones furnished by the car attendant.

In the lounge, which was still lighted, Christina saw a young woman of about her own age, coming up the snack bar stairwell carrying a box with snacks and paper cup. She smiled and said, "The snack bar is still open. I feel lucky."

"Good," said Christina. "I need some coffee too. I have extra sandwiches if you'd care to join me." They introduced themselves and the ensuing conversation resulted in an instant friendship as it revealed that they had much in common: newly graduated from high school, interested in Jane Austen, and both were headed for the Regency Seminar in Santa Fe. Jane Fairfax was her new friend's name, a pretty girl with wavy blonde hair, tall and graceful, with an air of genteel amiability. She was returning home to Santa Fe after a visit to her aunt in St. Louis.

"You'll be staying in a dorm?" she asked.

"No, my scholarship includes a boarding house near the campus. It's Mrs. Buttery's Cottage. Have you heard of it?"

"Indeed I have! Mrs. Buttery is the doyenne of Santa Fe society and runs the Cottage like an exclusive sorority. Some people say the Cottage is haunted, but I think that's a campus legend that people have spread. How did you obtain a scholarship for the seminar?"

Christina explained the struggle of the essay contest, the trauma of her loss, and the good fortune of her eventual award, ending with her admiration for her teachers, especially Mr. Saxon, who had been taken off the train with sudden illness.

"It sounds as if he won't be coming to Santa Fe. I wonder who will be teaching the history part of the seminar. I hope you can contact him. I hope he's O.K." Jane finished her sandwich, and their conversation continued with kindly interest and good will on the part of both, exchanging views on their favorite Austen heroes and books.

The hour grew late, and finally Christina remarked that she should go back to her seat with the obese snoring lady, or search for another vacant seat in her coach where she could get some sleep.

"I'm in a little roomette in the sleeper car," remarked Jane. "Why don't I have the car attendant arrange the upper bunk for you there. There's not a lot of room to change clothes, but you can at least stretch out and get some sleep."

Christina accepted her invitation gratefully, and explained that there was no need to change clothes. She followed Jane to the first-class car, removed her shoes and climbed up to the cozy shelf above Jane. Her exhaustion, the gentle swaying of the train, and the comfort of having found a friend, relaxed her immediately, and she fell asleep thinking, "A train is such a nice way to travel."

Chapter VIII

*...when we do return, it shall not
be like other travelers,...we will
know where we have gone.*

—Jane Austen

Her opinion of the suitability of train travel
was enhanced in the morning by the pleasure of
accompanying Jane to the dining car for a breakfast of French toast and bacon. The white table-
cloth, the shining silverware, and the yellow rose
bouquet gave an elegance to the table, and the
elderly couple who shared their table engaged
them in a pleasant conversation with inquiries
that seemed to include them as part of a gracious
society of cosmopolitan travelers.

The two young women returned to the lounge
car, where the seats facing the large windows gave

a more panoramic view of the western plains. Jane, having traveled the route many times, told Christina to watch for antelope and for the ruts of the Santa Fe Trail, the old wagon road that led traders to Santa Fe before the railroad made the Trail obsolete.

There was a long stop scheduled for La Junta, (Spanish for *The Junction*) Colorado, and because they had arrived early, passengers had a chance to stroll the platform or cross the street to visit some of the shops. Christina and Jane had coffee in the Copper Kettle Cafe, bought the local newspaper, and enjoyed the photos and ads for the Koshare Indian dances.

"Their faces look quite light. I always thought the Native Americans were quite dark skinned," Christina said.

"I think they're of all shades, just like the rest of us. Do you prefer light or dark skin for a man? Would you date a dark skinned man?"

"I don't think the color would matter as long as he can dance," Christina laughed.

"I agree," Jane replied. "But that is only a minimum requirement. I like a man who is a friendly talker. Last year I danced with a man at the Debutante Ball who was so handsome and graceful on the dance floor, but a stupid conversationalist. We sat out one dance together and he did not say one thing. I tried questions and small talk, but he answered only with yes or no. So dull and stupid."

"And he should have a sense of humor," added Christina.

"If that's important for you, you'll like my brother Tommy. He's the life of the party. Rather a rattle, and quite a tease, but good hearted. He's supposed to meet me at the station. He'll take you to Mrs. Buttery's. It's on the way to our house."

Christina learned that Jane had another brother also, much older, who taught economics in college and had his own apartment in Santa Fe, but her talk focused on Tommy, and the more Jane talked about Tommy, a great outdoorsman, ranch manager and horseman, the more Christina looked forward to meeting him.

"And he's neither dark, nor light, so you'd be a perfect match for him," Jane joked. As they boarded the train, she added, "I wish we could stay here longer and see Bent's Fort. It's not very far; it's an adobe reconstruction of the old trading post here in the 1800's. That's one of Tommy's favorite places. He'll tell you all about it."

Christina's first view of the mountains was the sight of snow-covered twin peaks on the horizon to the northwest. Looking at the travel guide booklet Jane showed her, she asked, "How do you pronounce that Indian name? It says here it means The Breasts of Mother Earth"

"We just call them the Spanish Peaks," Jane replied.

Suddenly the train began to slow and then came to a stop. Open country, no crossings, and no announcements left them wondering about the cause of the delay. A man in a seat near them said, "Probably another freight train. The freight companies own the tracks so they get the right of way, and passenger trains get the delay."

But no other train came by. Looking out the window Jane said, "There's a conductor or engineer going along as if checking the train or the tracks." As the train began to move, someone said,

"We hit some cows."

Looking out the window, Christina was horrified to see the mangled body of a huge animal, its blood and bones heaped close beside the train.

An announcement was made to the effect that two cows had been hit. The delay was due to a subsequent required inspection of the train to make sure all connections were secure. Moving on again, the train finally arrived in Trinidad, Colorado, a coal mining town. Fisher's Peak on the left, dominated the skyline.

As the train left Trinidad, Colorado, it began a slow climb up the steep Raton Pass, the highest point on the route of the trains bound for Santa Fe. A sign indicated an altitude of over 7,800 feet and proclaimed "The Site of Uncle Dick Wootten's Ranch."

"Is it a famous ranch? Why the big sign?" asked Christina.

"This is the Mountain Branch of the Santa Fe Trail. The Cimarron Route is shorter, but because of more Indian attacks on that Cutoff, the old traders often preferred this route. There's more water this way also. The Cimarron Route had a big dry stretch where animals and people could die trying to get across. But this Mountain Route was so steep the wagons had to be winched up a few yards at a time over the rocks. It was Uncle Dick Wootten who cleared a path and built a toll road, making it easier for the wagons to go this route. He charged everyone a toll, except the Indians."

Steep green banks with pine trees, and the public address announcement about watching for elk, kept them glued to the windows. Someone shouted, "Bears!" and a black bear with a cub following it went bounding up the cliff side. Then all went dark as the train entered a tunnel at the highest point of the pass.

Coming out of the tunnel, the train was now in New Mexico, and there was a short stop at the town of Raton. A group of Boy Scouts got off there, headed for Philmont Ranch, the National Center for Boy Scouts of America. "If we were going the other way, leaving Raton, you'd hear the boys who get on here telling about their first experience camping in the wilderness and dealing with the bears," Jane said.

Nearby passengers, hearing Jane explain points of interest, began asking questions. "Where does that Cutoff Trail join the main route? Is there a fort there? Can we see the Trail from the train?"

Jane explained that, although the Trail was not visible from the train, the two routes came together near the town of Watrous. "The train zips through the village of Springer. Look! There it is," she said. "But if we were riding in a car through here, we'd see signs telling us this is the junction of the two routes of the Trail. And to the west a few miles is Fort Union National Monument, the ruins of the old fort that was the supply center for all the forts of the Southwest."

"Look at that mountain," someone said. "It's shaped like a high-top shoe."

"The covered wagon travelers thought it resembled a wagon pulled by oxen," Jane explained. "The name of the town is Wagon Mound."

The conductor announced, "Las Vegas, next stop. If this is your destination, proceed to the lower level to de-train."

"Las Vegas?" someone asked. "Are we in Nevada?"

"No. This is Las Vegas, New Mexico. Las Vegas means 'The Meadows.' It was a wild town in the early days and now it's famous for its university, the beautiful Victorian houses, and the Casteñeda, which was a Harvey House. Harvey Houses were restaurant stops for the trains before they had dining cars. If you look out the window you'll see the brick arches of the Castañeda right near the tracks. It's been used as a setting in several movies." Jane was attracting a large audience with her tour-guide information.

After Las Vegas the train stopped again in a delay due to a freight train. Then nearing Lamy, their destination, the train made another halt to let the eastbound passenger train go by.

"We're so late," Jane said. "I hope Tommy doesn't mind waiting. Maybe he called the station to see if we're on time."

The little station with its Spanish arches and cottonwood trees was located in a valley fifteen miles south of Santa Fe. A crowd of people was waiting to board or to greet arriving passengers. But after getting off, claiming their luggage from the baggage cart, and looking inside the station, they saw no sign of Tommy. A call to Jane's house in Santa Fe brought no answer. The Santa Fe Chief train had moved on toward Albuquerque and Los Angeles, the crowd was gone, and even the Lamy taxi shuttle had left.

Jane said, "We're stranded!"

Chapter IX

*A college degree is a Social
Certificate, not a proof of
competence.*

—Elbert Hubbard

"What do we do now?" Christina thought Jane
looked quite calm, in spite of her declaration.

"We'll talk to Sandy. She'll know what's going
on."

Sandy, the friendly station agent, looked up
from her desk as the girls entered the waiting
room. "Hello, Jane. I have a message for you.
Your brother called. He said he couldn't meet you
today.

I told Tony he'd now have another passenger when he returned from Santa Fe. He was full

up with people from the eastbound train, but he should be back within the hour."

"Did Tommy say why he couldn't come?"

"No, and I didn't ask. It must be something came up suddenly because I didn't get the call until just before the train was due."

"Well, that's Tommy. He probably forgot. I love my brother, but he gets going on too many things at once, and forgets to put them in order of importance. At least, what's important to his sister," she added with a laugh.

While they waited, Jane took Christina across the road to the Legal Tender Restaurant, showed her the antique, hand-carved bar in the lobby and the plaques giving the history of the building. The present building replaced an earlier hotel which was a Harvey House like the Castañeda in Las Vegas.

While waiting for the taxi shuttle, the girls sat in the shade of the cottonwood trees near the station at a picnic table and talked about the coming summer. "We'll see each other in classes, I hope," said Jane. "But I want you to come to my house for dinner soon. And my eighteenth birthday is coming. I'm looking forward to a party, but I'm also worried about it."

"Why? Aren't your parents planning it, or is it supposed to be a surprise?"

"No, my mother said I could have a party, but she's been looking at me oddly and said some strange things a while ago that make me wonder if something else is going to happen."

Christina began to ask about the "strange things," but at that moment the taxi shuttle arrived and their attention shifted to getting their luggage aboard and greeting Tony.

Tony, the Taxi man, proved to be a personable and entertaining raconteur. He kept copies of several books by local authors on his dashboard and began boasting about Santa Fe and the number of celebrities living there. "Here's a book about Marc Simmons, the famous historian."

Because the two girls were his only two passengers, he focused his attention on them with friendly banter, and when he found that Christina was new to the Southwest, regaled them with exaggerated stories and dire warnings about entering Santa Fe.

"Yes," he explained, "this town has strange vibrations. Crystal gazers, mind readers, artists who paint crazy pictures that look like nightmares. Some of the statues are very interesting, but some will shock you. Jane can hold her hand over your eyes as we go past them. And there are ghosts galore. You're going to live at the Buttery Cottage? Well, don't take a room on the third floor. Look, here's a book telling about a nearby hotel, *The Adobe Castle,*" and he held up a little brown paperback. "That hotel is also haunted, for sure."

"Tony, you are such a joker," Jane put in. "Christina, he helps all the local authors by recommending their books, and he thinks he'll get bigger tips if he scares his passengers, or makes them laugh."

"Well, look there," he said as they pulled up to a large Victorian mansion. "Doesn't that look haunted? There's your Buttery Cottage. All the newer buildings have to be built in Pueblo or Territorial style, but this one is so old, it was put up before the town got regulated. You'll hear about the murders. Just remember what I told you about staying away from the third floor!"

Tony carried her bags to the front door, and bade her goodbye as the door opened. His haste in leaving was perhaps due to the glaring look from the woman who stood there, Mrs. Buttery herself. She motioned for Christina to enter, put on her pince-nez, and looked her up and down coldly.

"Dashwood? I don't recall a reservation for anyone by that name. Let me look at my register." Mrs. Buttery was large around the middle, but her legs were very thin, and as she walked, she gave the impression of a strutting hen. After consulting a large leather register, she returned to say, "I'm afraid, my Dear, that you've come to the wrong place. You may use the telephone here to call another hotel and a taxi to take you there."

At that, she pointed to the phone, and leaving Christina standing by her bags, marched through a distant archway, closing the door beyond it with an air of finality.

Chapter X

*Let us speak plain; there is more
force in names than most men
dream of.*

—JAMES RUSSELL LOWELL

What does a heroine do in such a discouraging situation?

Christina stood in shock for a few moments. Her first thought was to call Jane, but she realized she did not have her new friend's address or phone number. There was no phone book near the telephone. She decided to call the information operator hoping there would not be multiple listings for the name Fairfax. As she picked up the phone, she saw a notice on the wall above it.

NO LONG DISTANCE CALLS
LIMIT YOUR CALLS TO FIVE MINUTES

THIS PHONE IS TURNED OFF AT 9 P.M.

The clock above the telephone showed five minutes after nine. The situation seemed impossible. Her disappointment gradually turned to indignation at the woman who had so summarily dismissed her. She walked through the imposing arch to the doorway beyond and knocked on the door loudly. "Mrs. Buttery? Please listen to me. I'm sure I have a reservation. Let me show you my credentials. Here is a paper my teacher Mr. Saxon gave me. It has your name and the address of this house."

The door opened slowly, and Mrs. Buttery, clad in a short purple dressing gown, looked out and said, "Saxon? You said Saxon? Why did you not give me that name at the beginning? Let me look at the register again."

Looking more annoyed than apologetic Mrs. Buttery consulted the register again, acknowledged her error, and muttered something about now having to find another guest for the exchange dinner. She led Christina up a wide carpeted stairway, listing in a clipped tone the rules of the house as they ascended. "Breakfast is at seven. We are all women here, but you are to be fully dressed. No pajamas. No hair in curlers. Curfew is at ten p.m. for freshmen. Quiet hours begin at nine, and..," She stopped on the landing, quite out of breath, and after a moment explained that Christina could go on up to the third floor by herself and find the last room at the far end of the hall.

Christina herself was out of breath from climbing the long stairway while carrying her heavy bags. Jane had warned her that she would have to become acclimated to the high altitude. And here she was to have a room on the very third floor that Tony had warned against! She groped for a light switch and not finding one, trudged along in the dark to the last door and succeeded in finding a switch to light the tiny room that she entered.

Everything inside the room seemed miniature, as if designed for a child, but the bed looked adequate, the sheets were crisp and clean, and without examining any further, she undressed and climbed in. If there were creaking of stairways, wailing of ghosts, or luminescent apparitions that night, Christina, in her exhaustion and relief at having finally arrived, slept unaware of them and so soundly that she did not waken till the breakfast bell rang.

There was the sound of running footsteps from the floor below. She suddenly realized that the other girls must be running to breakfast, or leaving for classes. Becoming fully awake, unpacking far enough to find her toiletries kit and a robe, then searching for the bathroom down the hall, took considerable time. And by the time she was fully dressed and ready for breakfast, she descended to find the breakfast room empty except for Mrs. Buttery and a short, plump lady in a green smock whom she took to be the maid. Mrs. Buttery was having coffee and a cigarette. She frowned with disapproval at Christina.

"You must learn to be more prompt, my Dear. Sit here and do not slouch. No elbows or arms on the table. Sara, bring more toast and see if there is enough coffee left. I will explain about the exchange dinner. Once a month five of our girls attend dinner at the Rho Sigma House, and five of their boys come to Buttery Cottage. It is a practice in social dining and polite conversation."

At this point, the phone rang and Christina was glad for the interruption so she could begin eating. When Mrs. Buttery returned to the table, she announced, "You will dine here, and your guest at dinner will be Tommy Fairfax. I don't know where he came from because when I called last night they said no one else was available, but our numbers will be even now. Please dress appropriately. The Rho Sigma boys always wear shirts, ties, and jackets for dinner." She took up her coffee cup, lighted another cigarette and ended the instructions.

Tommy Fairfax! How did he belong to Rho Sigma House? Jane had said her brother stayed mostly at the ranch, and was not taking any summer courses. Did Jane learn about the dinner and somehow get Tommy on the invitation list? She hoped she would see Jane at registration, and looking at the clock, realized she was due at registration an hour ago. Gulping her coffee, she remembered to say, "May I please be excused, Mrs. Buttery? I fear I am late," and not waiting for a reply, she headed for the door, without knowing which way she should go.

Other students on the street directed her to the Administration Building where she filled out the necessary papers, and then headed across the campus to Simmons Hall, for her first class, History of England.

The low adobe building opened on a wide hall which seemed to be empty. She ran along the hall, passing several open doors with empty rooms. Then hearing the authoritative voice of a teacher proclaiming, "The young Henry the Eighth was a popular king," she guessed that classroom would be hers and she entered hesitantly, pausing just inside the door to catch her breath. The short bearded man interrupted his lecture, glared at

her, and in a stern voice said, "Miss Dashwood?"
Her faint acknowledgement was followed by his
sarcastic, "You will have to dash faster, if you are
to be on time in this class. You may now dash up
to your seat here in the first row."

Snickers of amusement followed her progress
to the front of the room, and as she took the empty seat, she stumbled and dropped her notebook
with a loud clatter, eliciting more chuckles.

No heroine could be more ill at ease on the
first day of her summer adventure. Acute nostal-
gia for home swept over her.

Where was Jane? The professor had evidently
given his lecture many times before, and his delivery was a memorized recitation, delivered in a
pontifical voice as he marched around the room.
He carried several long pieces of chalk, which he
juggled from hand to hand as he strode. Some
students became fascinated with his perfor-
mance, while others took notes furiously, heads
bent over their notebooks. Taking advantage of
watching him, Christina was able to turn and sur-
vey the classroom behind her, but did not see
Jane, who must have been assigned to a different
section of the class.

Chapter XI

*Repartee is what you wish you'd
said.*

—HEYWOOD BROUN

The Regency Seminar was held in the middle of the regular summer term of the Santa Fe Villa Real College. Because the history class had already been in session, Christina was at a disadvantage in entering a class in which students were already prepared. This fact became evident as the professor halted at the front of the room, and pointing at Christina demanded, "How many of his six wives did Henry the Eighth execute?"

Christina, in embarrassed confusion, tried to recall the words of Jane Austen's juvenile book titled *The History of England by a partial,*

prejudiced, and ignorant Historian. All she recalled was that the satirical chapter on Henry VIII
had included the line, "The Crimes & Cruelties of
this Prince, were too numerous to be mentioned,"
and she answered, "All of them?'"

More laughter from the class, and the professor said, "*Divorced, beheaded, died. Divorced
beheaded, survived.* Remember that, Miss Dashwood, for recall on the next quiz." And he continued his circuit of the room, telling about the
dissolution of the monasteries. He stopped next
to another student who was busily working the
crossword puzzle in the Campus News and said,
"Number thirteen Down is IRONY, a good term to
remember."

At the front of the room he began to place
the sticks of chalk on end along the narrow ridge
at the top of the lectern, intoning all the while
about the Reformation, and creating suspense as
to whether the chalk pieces would fall, domino
fashion. At that moment Christina saw his name
behind him, written on the blackboard. Doctor
John Barber. So this was the infamous professor Jane had told her about! Admired by some,
held in awe by others, and hated by the rest. She
turned to a fresh page in her notebook and wrote,
"Being a BARBER gives him the right to CUT
down ignorant students, doesn't it!"

The dark haired boy sitting next to her, smiled as he saw the note, and at that instant, Dr. Barber, making another circuit of the room, stopped behind her and reading the note aloud, drew laughter from the class again, this time at his own expense.

"Touché, Miss Dashwood. That score is in your favor, and we'll look forward to the next round on Wednesday." Then sweeping the row of chalk pieces deftly into his briefcase, he said, "Read Chapter Eleven next. Class dismissed." And he strode from the room before the students could.

Christina was surrounded by smiling classmates and praised for her successful written repartee. She left the classroom in greatly improved spirits, deciding that her summer would be better than she had first determined.

Chapter XII

My idea of good company—is the company of clever, well-informed people, who have a great deal of conversation.

—JANE AUSTEN

Christina, hurrying across campus to meet Jane at the Student Center as they had previously arranged, was accosted by the dark-haired boy who had sat next to her. "Hi! I'm Ricardo Muñeca, the one who sits next to you. Do you mind if I talk to you?"

"Oh, hello. No, that's fine. I'm on my way to meet a friend.

You're welcome to join us."

As they walked, the conversation revealed that he was from Albuquerque, a freshman

majoring in literature, and hoping to recruit students for the newly-formed Lit Club. Christina revealed that her short seminar course left no time
for extra-curricular activities, but she expressed
interest in the activities it involved, so as to seek
out a similar club when she returned to her college in Michigan.

They arrived at the Student Center and found
Jane sitting with Danielle, a petite brunette with
large blue eyes. After introductions and Coke
orders, the conversation turned lively with Ricardo's telling of the Dr. Barber incident, Jane's
amused reaction, and their tales of other instructors. Danielle and Ricardo soon left for their next
class, and Christina was finally able to make her
phone call home with the news of her arrival
and first morning at college. Her parents were in
touch with Mr. Saxon and reported that his in-
disposition had been of minor concern and that
he had plans to travel to Santa Fe later in the
summer.

Christina and Jane enjoyed further talk.
"Where did you find such a cute hunk of a man?"
Jane asked. "You're doing great for your first day
of classes! I heard from Tommy. He had a good
excuse for not meeting us at Lamy. His prize
mare was about to foal, and now has the prettiest
little filly you can imagine. I'm looking forward to

taking you up to the ranch to see all the horses. And you'll see Tommy tonight for sure. One of the Rho Sigma boys called him to be the dinner partner of the new girl at Buttery Cottage, and of course, that's you!"

Christina related the news she had already learned at Buttery Cottage, and the two girls went off to Jane Austen class together, with high anticipation of finding it their favorite.

They were not disappointed. Their instructor was Doctor Jean Roy, author of the text for the class, *Jane Austen for the Uninformed*. Dr. Roy was a lively, voluble speaker and her cheerful interaction with the students resulted in stimulating conversations.

She began with "I assume you have heard of Jane Austen, even if you haven't read any of her books. Maybe you've seen a film based on one of her books and are wondering why the big fuss about a romance writer who lived over two hundred years ago. At the very least, you do not confuse Jane Austen with Jane Eyre, which is a book written by a different author. In this class you will learn about the society Jane Austen lived in, the rules by which the gentry lived, and her influence in today's world.

"Tomorrow you will attend dancing class, so I will warn you now not to dance with the same gentleman more than twice. And you gentlemen, remember it is your duty to see that each young lady without a partner is asked to dance."

There followed a lively discussion comparing today's line dancing, square dancing, gyrations of singles on the dance floor, and questions about why the waltz was considered a sinful activity and actually horrified the gentry when it was first introduced in 1812.

The class ended on a merry note of expectation and lively talk, with only a few of the boys grumbling, "Gloves? We need white gloves for gym class?"

Christina and Jane rushed to the bookstore to buy their copies of the textbook, and thence to the library to begin reading about the scandalous waltz, but instead ended up discussing what they would wear to dancing class. For Christina, her more immediate concern was which frock she would wear to this evening's exchange dinner.

"That's one disadvantage of living at home instead of being in a dorm or boarding house," complained Jane. "If I knew more of the boys in Rho Sigma, or some of the girls in Buttery Cottage, I probably would be invited."

"If there's another exchange dinner before the end of summer, I'll get you invited for sure," countered Christina.

Chapter XIII

There is, I believe, in many men,
especially single men, such an
inclination—such a passion for
dining out—a dinner engagement
is so high in the class of their
pleasures, their employments,
their dignities, almost their duties,
that any thing gives way to it.

—JANE AUSTEN

The dining room of Buttery Cottage that evening was aglow with candle light, shining silver, Haviland china, and the quiet conversation of young men and women on their best behavior. Mrs. Buttery presided at the head of the long table with all the majesty of a monarch, stiff and erect in her high-backed chair, and frowning at the empty chair on her left.

Next to that chair was Christina, prettily coifed with a rose in her hair, but with a worried expression. Tommy Fairfax was late.

Mrs. Buttery had delayed ringing the bell for the beginning of the first course, but now announced, "We shall wait only three more minutes for our absent guest before we begin."

Ricardo, sitting across from Christina, said, "Maybe he can't find a complete shirt." There was laughter, and prompted by another boy to tell the story of the incomplete shirt, Ricardo explained that last year, Tommy, contriving to circumvent the rules of the dormitory dress code, kept one jacket to which was attached only the top of a shirt with a bow tie attached. He had sewn white cuffs to the inside of the jacket and wore it only for dinner, removing it as soon as he returned to his room. On one very warm night at dinner a fellow student had dared him to take off his jacket. Encouraged by the dares and with money accumulating on a bet that he actually would or would not, Tommy had risen, had removed his jacket, and had stood with his bare chest on display, topped by only the little bib with its bow tie.

Laughter followed. Mrs. Buttery frowned. Then the door opened and Tommy himself swept into the room. With big strides he hurried to the table, bowed before Mrs. Buttery, and handed her a hostess gift, a tiny box wrapped in gold paper.

"Please excuse my late arrival," he said. "I was held up by a stalled logging truck on the winding road with no way to pass. I regret making you delay the dinner."

And turning to Christina, he said, "This must be the fair Christina. I am pleased to meet you. My sister told me I would have the best looking girl as my dinner date." His wide smile, warm voice and ingratiating manner melted Mrs. Buttery's cold demeanor. And the welcoming comments of his friends with comments about his jacket, set the room at ease. The dinner was served in a merry atmosphere.

Tommy's blond hair was tousled, and his tanned face was red with exertion, giving credence to his delay. His suede jacket was worn over a silk vest and blue western shirt. The boys teased him by asking if the ensemble was really in separate pieces, and joshed him about trying to look like a fancy dude. But his popularity was evidenced mostly with his winning manners that captivated the doughty Mrs. Buttery. Most of the boarders knew little of Mrs. Buttery's past. Some speculated that she had been a sergeant in the WACs during the war. Others said she was the former matron of a women's prison. Tommy, with his clever compliments on the china and inquiries about its origins, soon learned the story of her past occupation.

"Yes, this is English china, imported by Mr. Fred Harvey," she explained. "Being one of the Harvey Girls when the Belen Harvey House closed, I was privileged to buy it."

"Who were the Harvey Girls?" someone asked.

"We were waitresses in the restaurants along the Santa Fe Railroad before the trains had dining cars. Only the best food was prepared by the best chefs, and served in the proper manner. The restaurants began with men as waiters, but when Mr. Harvey came to the Raton Hotel one day with a surprise inspection and found the men absent and injured after a brawl, he fired everyone, including the manager. The new manager decided that women would be more dependable and Mr. Harvey advertised for young women between 18 and 30, intelligent, and with high morals, to be trained as waitresses. We had to sign a contract with strict rules."

"No flirting with the customers?"

"We had to remain single for the duration of our contract, live in women's dormitories in the hotels, keep curfew hours, wear special uniforms, and follow the serving protocol of European establishments."

As the interested company followed the story and enjoyed the courses that Sara served, Christina gloried in her luck at having the most handsome and charming gentleman as her dinner partner.

Our heroine believed that she had found her hero.

Chapter XIV

Suspicion often creates what it suspects.

—C.S.LEWIS

Though believing she had found her hero, Christina was not sure her hero felt that he had found his heroine. Her first feeling of uneasiness in that regard surfaced when he had looked down the opposite side of the table and locked gazes with the attractive blonde girl in the shimmering green dress. She was Mary Sidney, Christina's rival in the essay contest!

On first entering the dining room, Christina and Mary had recognized and greeted each other excitedly. Christina began to tell Mary about her train journey and the departure of Mr. Saxon, but

Mary coolly responded that she already knew. "Fibrillation. They're controlling it with medication. He's O.K. He'll be back here for end of term." And Mary continued telling of her own flight, followed by the ride from Albuquerque with a General Somebody, and other passengers who were important scientists on their way to Los Alamos, the Secret City of the Manhattan Project. "And when I got here I had an invitation to a rush party for the Kit Kat Club. That's the Santa Fe Sorority for college freshmen. I don't know how they got my name. I really should have brought more clothes. I went shopping with Danielle yesterday, but couldn't find a thing I liked. All so Southwestern with flounces and scarves. I did find this turquoise and silver bracelet in a little shop on the plaza. Do you like it?" And she held out her arm for Christina to admire and respond with compliments.

"It's very pretty." Christina replied. "Are you living in the dorm? How did you get invited to this Buttery Cottage dinner?"

"Lucy Van Mortelle is my dorm roommate. Her brother is in Rho Sigma. I guess it's a matter of knowing the right people."

The dinner ended with a delicious flan dessert, the smooth southwestern style custard with caramel glaze. The diners wanted to applaud the cook, and called for Sara, who responded by peeking out from the kitchen and waving a dish-towel. Mrs. Buttery waved no towel, but with her hand dismissed the ladies and gentlemen with kind words which implied that the evening was at an end.

The boys soon began moving toward the door, some shaking hands with their dinner part-ners and making plans to meet in the future. But Tommy and Ricardo, enjoying their conversa-tion with Christina and Danielle, lingered in the front parlor which served as a living room and foyer. Christina observed that Mary held out her hand to Tommy in leaving, but it was impossible to detect whose fault it was that the handclasp was sustained longer than is customary. Tommy sat down on the sofa near the door and asked Christina another question about her Michigan home, and she took a seat next to him. Danielle and Ricardo carried on their conversation on the loveseat nearby, and soon they were the only two couples left, even after the dining room was cleared and darkened.

"Yes, we had one horse, but Lilly and I did not ride. My father used the horse for cultivating corn."

"You had no tractor?"

"Oh, yes, a 1918 Fordson. But we live next to a mink farm, and the owner requested that we use the horse on the field next to the mink cages, so the noisy tractor would not disturb the mink who were having babies."

"Wow!" exclaimed Ricardo. "Was that the old crank-up affair with the metal wheels?"

While Christina nodded and explained further, Tommy looked through the dining room arch at the door beyond, which was the entrance to Mrs. Buttery's apartment. The door was slightly ajar, and he could dimly discern a figure in the darkened room beyond. Changing the subject, and at the same time, catching Ricardo's eye and nodding his head sideways as if pointing toward that door, he asked, "Have you ever read Cooper's *The Spy?*"

Ricardo caught his meaning and replied, "Bunch of rot. I wouldn't recommend it to anyone." Danielle giggled and Christina did not understand, until she saw Ricardo take Danielle's hand in both of his and saw that the door opened a wee bit farther. Mrs. Buttery was surreptitiously guarding her charges as if they were her Harvey Girls in danger of the advances of western ruffians!

Tommy smiled and took up the game of teasing by putting his arm on the back of the sofa and lowering it slightly till it was almost around Christina's shoulder. At that moment, the door opened and Mrs. Buttery emerged with a loud cough, and marched toward the kitchen. When she returned with a glass of water, she closed the door firmly, as if reminding them that the hour was late and the cozy couples' situations should proceed no further.

But shortly, they saw that the door was ajar again, and evidently enjoying the game, Tommy took Christina's hand in his and drew it toward his lips. At that moment Mrs. Buttery emerged the second time and pointing to the clock said, "It is after nine-thirty. You must have studies to complete, Gentlemen. I must bid you good night."

The gentlemen acquiesced politely, and still smiling, Tommy pressed both of Christina's hands in his own and bade her good night with hopes of seeing her soon at the Fairfax Ranch.

Ricardo gave an equally cordial greeting to Danielle and with a slight bow, the two gentlemen departed.

Danielle giggled all the way up the stairs, but Christina, although enjoying the joke, and realizing that Tommy's handclasp was only for teasing under the watchful eye of Mrs. Buttery, was entertained by more than the humor. She loved having Tommy look into her eyes as he held her hands and was grateful that the handclasp had lasted longer than the one between him and Mary Sidney.

She fell asleep and dreamed of handsome cowboys wearing suede jackets with blue shirts, riding huge black stallions across the New Mexico desert. But as many dreams do, this one ended in an embarrassing or awkward situation for the dreamer. She found herself only half dressed and standing behind a piñon tree as the horses thundered past. Where were her clothes? She was going to a formal ball and was in a terrible state of dishabille. She awoke with a start. The noise of the horses' hooves gave way to loud footsteps in the hallway. Frightened, she turned on a light. The sound receded, but the rest of the night she slept only fitfully with a mixture of happy hopes and vague fears.

Chapter XV

Every savage can dance.

—JANE AUSTEN

The next day was dancing class. Christina, Mary, and Danielle, eager to begin, arrived at the hall before the scheduled time and were rewarded with a special private demonstration by the dance master and his partner, who were enjoying a graceful gallop around the empty room. They were dipping, swirling, almost leaping in coordinated cadences, until suddenly aware of the audience and the clock, they stopped abruptly and bowed as if to an audience of hundreds. The three girls stood in awe, then clapped politely.

"That was beautiful!" Christina exclaimed. "But was that the sinful waltz? It looked more like flying angels."

Dance Master Solier was dark, thin, and graceful, but a large mole to the left of his mouth gave him a rather forbidding appearance. His partner was equally dark, thin, and graceful, but with a younger and sweeter expression. An interesting birthmark near her chin gave her an exotic look. As more students entered the hall, the dance master stood stiffly before them, rapped sharply on the floor with a long staff, and called for attention.

"I am Monsieur Solier. This is Madame Solier. We will introduce you to Eighteenth Century dance, beginning with the Pavanne and Minuet, and ending with English Contredanse. Gentlemen are to wear gloves, ladies, long skirts. Absolute silence during instruction. Conversation at designated intervals."

Jane whispered to Christina, "His real name is Señor Salazar. James told me. But he wants to appear French. He thinks it's more elegant."

"How does James know that?"

"Faculty gossip. All the instructors know each other."

Monsieur and Madame lined the students up single file and paraded them around the room under sharp scrutiny. After the second circuit, Monsieur halted them and rapped his staff sharply on the floor.

"You should be ashamed! I have never seen a more graceless or gauche assembly. You are ladies and gentlemen of the Royal Court, not clodhoppers! Stand tall. Chins up. Slower steps. Smooth. Do not bounce. Stay an arm's length behind the person in front of you," And he tapped his rod at lengthy intervals to indicate the steps.

Christina noticed a small group of men standing in the doorway, watching their efforts with amused expressions. One tall man in a dark suit seemed searching for someone in the class as he eyed the passing line. Was it her imagination, or did his gaze seem to follow her especially? She stole glances at him as the line advanced toward the door.

Monsieur Solier stopped the parade and asked the ladies and gentlemen to take seats on opposite sides of the room. As he began explaining the proper protocol for asking and refusing a partner, he turned to the watchers in the doorway and said, "When the number of ladies exceeds the number of gentlemen at an assembly ball, it is rude to stand watching without asking a lady to dance. Please have a seat, Gentlemen, as I explain how you can accommodate us here."

Two of the watchers shuffled in slowly and took seats, but the tall man, after glancing at his watch, quickly disappeared with the rest.

Monsieur Solier, after pairing the couples to his satisfaction, introduced them to the Pavanne, a slow and stately dance with advances, curtseys, bowing, and retreats. When they turned and marched as pairs, the lady rested her hand on the back of the gentleman's hand.

Now they were finally moving to music, along with Monsieur's tapping staff. Christina's partner was Ricardo. At first, he seemed happy to be dancing with her, but his eager steps did not match the rhythm of the music. Could he not hear the beat? His jerking movements made for such awkward progress that they drew the attention of Monsieur Solier who approached them and counted aloud while tapping his staff. His attention only increased the couple's discomfiture and threw them more off rhythm. Ricardo was perspiring visibly, and Christina's face felt flushed. She longed for the end of the dance and hoped that she could have a different partner. Could Tommy Fairfax be this graceless? Jane, marching along behind and sometimes near to her side, must have been reading her thoughts because she said, "I'm glad Tommy isn't here. He's a good square dancer, but he would laugh at this slow Pavanne."

The class finally ended, to Christina's great relief, and as they walked along the hall she learned that the tall man who had been standing in the doorway was Jane's brother James! "He was watching us," Jane explained. "I had described you and he was watching to see which one you were. He's quite shy."

"He looked at his watch, and then left." Christina said. "He's very nice looking, but he must be quite a bit older than you and Tommy."

"Yes, and you'll get to meet him soon if you accept my invitation to come home with me for the weekend. We'll have supper at our house here in Santa Fe and go up to the ranch on Saturday. Do say you will. We'll have such fun!"

Christina accepted with alacrity and that night dreamed about both of the brothers. Blond Tommy and dark-haired James were marching in single file with Tommy in the lead. Monsieur Solier was marching behind them and tapping his staff with such audible beats that she woke suddenly and the vision vanished. The tapping was actually loud footsteps. They seemed to be coming, not from the hallway, but from overhead. Was there an attic above her room? Was someone walking on the roof? She sat up and listened as the sound faded and finally ceased. Then anticipation of the coming weekend superseded any fear of ghosts, and she slept soundly till morning.

Chapter XVI

*To keep up and improve
Friendship, thou must be willing
to receive a Kindness, as well as to
do one.*

—Thomas Fuller

Jane's house was within walking distance of the Buttery Cottage, where Jane met Christina and helped her carry her books and overnight bag to the Fairfax home. They crossed the Plaza, a pleasant tree-lined square with shops on three sides and the pueblo style Palace of the Governors on the fourth side, where Indians were selling their jewelry and pots displayed on colorful blankets. Past the huge Cathedral, the streets were narrow with high adobe walls close to the sidewalk. Were there no yards with lawns?

Christina felt as if she were in a foreign land. The glare and heat in the narrow street became excessive. Finally they came to a huge gate with a wooden double door, which Jane pushed open to reveal another low adobe wall. But beyond that wall was a huge patio garden with a fountain and a profusion of colorful blossoming plants. A path led to a low portico, which gave entrance to the dining room of the house, cool, dim, and elegant in contrast to the street.

Jane's mother, a dark, handsome woman, greeted them graciously and showed Christina a room where she could freshen up and rest until dinner. "We're so glad you could come. Jane has found a good friend." Mrs. Fairfax spoke with a Spanish accent which added to her exotic charm.

"Will James get here in time for dinner?" Jane asked. "He's been admiring Christina at a distance and wants to meet her."

"He's been very busy with paperwork for his classes, but he told me he would try to come," Mrs. Fairfax replied.

James lived at a faculty club, but dined with his family once or twice a week. Jane explained that two other members of the household were Maria, who would be serving dinner, and her husband José, whom they would meet at the ranch tomorrow.

Maria rang a little bell, and James appeared in time to hold the chair and seat his mother. Then, turning to Jane he said, "You must introduce me formally to your friend. I heard your dancing teacher say that there must be an introduction before two people could dance together."

"Yes, and you left the dance assembly room before you could be introduced," Jane laughed.

"I was almost late for my class. I did enjoy watching all you lovely ladies try to herd a bunch of gawky college boys around the room," he replied.

After Jane made the introduction, James leaned forward with almost a formal bow and extended his hand to Christina. His polite formality made Christina's face feel hot, and Jane said, "You've made her blush!"

Maria entered with a huge pot of green chili chicken soup, and the dinner continued in silence as they enjoyed the spicy viands. As the next course was being served, the phone rang, and James left the room to answer it. When he returned, he called his mother to the phone. When she returned, she looked rather disconcerted, and her face was pale.

"Is everything O.K. at the ranch?" Jane asked.

"Yes, but we now have two extra guests, a couple from England, so I must add to Maria's list for tomorrow."

Jane explained that the Fairfax Ranch sometimes took in travelers and, although never advertised, was known as a guest ranch. Christina noticed Mrs. Fairfax often glancing at Jane with a worried look during the rest of the meal. What could it mean, wondered Christina. Jane seemed oblivious to her mother's change of mood, and expressed happiness that there would be additional visitors.

James excused himself before dessert with apologies for leaving early due to his stack of waiting paperwork. "I may try to join you at the ranch tomorrow for supper, if I can," he said.

After dinner Jane and Christina settled in the large living room to work on their homework, especially the paper due Monday for the Austen class. An essay titled "The Carriage and The Young Man Who Will Drive It" was to be explained as if an afternoon date were being arranged between two people in the late Eighteenth Century in the English countryside. Jane had brought her textbook which listed the various kinds of carriages and the class of people associated with each. They enjoyed great merriment in the speculation of their choice of young man and the descriptions of the Coach, Curricle, Gig, Phaeton, and Barouche.

"It says here," said Jane, "that you are what you drive. Just like today with different kinds of cars for the sporty or the show-offs, or people who are practical and the slow drivers. I would want to be driven in a big barouche landau with white horses."

"I'll take a jaunting cart," said Christina, "as long as the gentleman is the proper breed."

Their laughter and talk continued late into the evening with very little writing accomplished, but the session further enhanced the enjoyment of their companionship and cemented their friendship.

Alone in her room later, Christina wondered about the disturbing phone call. Surely the coming of additional guests in a country hotel should not cause the owners that much unease and bring about the change she had noticed in the demeanor of James and his mother. Would tomorrow reveal the reason?

Chapter XVII

*Life is either a daring adventure
or nothing.*

—HELEN KELLER

In the morning with the station wagon all loaded, Jane and Christina, with Mrs. Fairfax and Maria, set off for the ranch. The paved streets gave way to gravel roads as the piñon pines gave way to ponderosas, and the road became steeper. They emerged from the forest to see a vast expanse of grass, backed by more forested mountains.

"This is the Valles Caldera," Jane explained. "It's actually the crater of an extinct volcano. We bring the cattle up here in spring to graze for the summer and take them down in the fall."

Christina had to adjust her perception of the
view as she realized the tiny dots near the far
edge of the meadows were actually cattle. And
the ranch buildings she saw in the distance
were four miles away! No Michigan landscapes
stretched the eyesight so far as this one did.

The ranch and its outbuildings were made of
logs. The two story structure was shaped like
a giant horseshoe with its opening toward the
mountains. "Just like the old inn yards of England
that Mr. Saxon told us about," declared Christina.

"Some of the upstairs rooms are for guests,
but the cabins you see out there are separate
guest rooms also," said Jane. "Daddy has his office in that little cabin over there because Mother doesn't like him to smoke in the house." As
they approached the main house, they saw a
uniformed chauffeur polishing a large black car
in the driveway, and later found out that the expected couple was actually the Englishman and
his American driver.

In the living room they met the English guest,
a pale middle-aged gentleman of average height
named Cecil Morgan. Thinning hair and a reced-
ing chin did him no credit, but his blue eyes behind round glasses and his cordial manner were
quite ingratiating.

Mrs. Fairfax engaged him in conversation while Jane took Christina to meet her father in his cabin office.

Mr. Fairfax, a burly light-haired gentleman, greeted Christina warmly and apologized for Tommy's absence. "He's riding fence over east of here, but he'll be back before supper and show you the horses."

Inside the house, Jane gave Christina a tour, stopping at her parents' bedroom to show its unusual feature, a tree growing from the floor and up through the second story. The trunk was decorated with family photos. "This is our family tree," explained Jane. "The older photos up there are my grandparents. That's why they're up at the top. And next are my parents, then James, Tommy and I when we were little kids."

"Who is that lady?" Christina asked, pointing to a photo of a beautiful woman with large dark eyes and a pageboy coiffure.

"That's my aunt Phyllida. She's not really my aunt, but she stayed here a lot many years ago and was my mother's best friend.

I don't remember her because she died when I was just little."

The room above, where the tree probably continued toward the roof, was a storage room. Christina wondered about how the branches were decorated there, but Jane did not offer to show it to her, merely explaining that it was just a thinner part of the trunk with no branches and had been cut off below the ceiling.

"But let's go upstairs now, and I'll show you your room. We have some time to get ready for supper, and maybe finish our Austen assignment too."

On the second level, the various rooms were labeled above each door with the name of a western trail: The Old Spanish Trail, The California Trail, El Camino Real, and the Lewis and Clark Trail. Her room was The Santa Fe Trail room, and inside, the furnishings carried out the theme with a bedstead made from a Murphy wagon wheel, a model of a covered wagon on top of the dresser and on the wall, a map of the Trail next to a scene of prairie grass with wagon wheel ruts extending far into the distance. Her window overlooked the circular drive approach, and beyond it she could see the vast meadow of grass backed by the distant ponderosa covered mountains. Christina was enchanted, but the setting kept her far away from Regency England with no desire to do her homework. Still gazing out the window, she saw a horse and rider approaching across the meadow. Could it be Tommy?

She ran down to see, and as she approached the gate, she saw that it was indeed her cowboy hero, looking rather tired and dusty, but strong and manly. His copper colored horse had a delicate head that bobbed rhythmically with each step. He reined in the horse, dismounted and greeted her. "Hi, Tina! Has Jane showed you the new baby? Come over and let's have a look."

Maria's husband, José, was cleaning the stables. He was introduced to Christina and accompanied them to the new mother and baby. In the stable the black mare stood guard over her little foal who moved on spindly legs looking shyly at them and peeking around her mother. Both had identical white blazes down the face. Christina and Tommy moved closer, but the mare, seeing a stranger, put her ears back and walked in a circle, protecting her little one. "It's O.K, Dulce, Tina's a friend. No fear, but we'll not bother you now," he said, and led the admiring Christina away to see the other horses. "Here's Brownie. He's old, fat and gentle. He'll be your horse for our ride tomorrow. Jane has Delicado, and we'll put that British dude on Jasper with an English saddle."

"Where are we going?"

"To Sotherton Abbey, of course!"

"There is no Sotherton Abbey! You've heard Jane talking about our Austen classes."

"Isn't an abbey an old religious building of some sort? I guarantee you'll see an abbey. This will be your first adventure at Fairfax Ranch."

Chapter XVIII

*It is a truth universally
acknowledged, that a single man
in possession of a good fortune,
must be in want of a wife.*

—JANE AUSTEN

The group that gathered around the supper table that evening evinced at first an air of general good will with polite inquiries regarding each other's home locations, travel plans, and preferences for the next day's activity. The meal began with a pleasant feeling, but in spite of the satisfaction afforded by the delicious chicken enchiladas, there seemed underneath to be an awkward and strangely troubled atmosphere.

Mr. and Mrs. Fairfax sat at the head and foot of the table, smiled at each other, and assumed the demeanor of gracious hosts.

Christina sat quietly with her hands in her lap shyly waiting for Mrs. Fairfax to lift her fork as the signal that the diners could begin. Mr. Morgan snapped open his napkin with a flourish and spread it across his knees, looking toward the kitchen in anticipation of the meal. His driver companion, a corpulent older gentleman named Mr. Thorp, tucked his napkin into his vest below his chin and rubbed his hands together in expectation of a spicy feast. James smiled across at Christina and asked if she had finished her homework. Jane and Tommy glanced at each other with a secret smile as if about to present a surprise. Then Tommy tapped a knife on his glass to draw everyone's attention for an announcement.

"Tomorrow's program is a trip to Sotherton Abbey. There are horses enough for everyone. So who wants to go?"

Mr. Fairfax said, "Tommy, you're not planning one of those wild rides over on the canyon ridge, are you?" And waving his arms in wide gestures he added, "Last time you scared the bejeebers out of those ladies from New York. I thought we'd have to order smelling salts from town, if you keep doing trips like that."

"No, Dad, this trip is to Sotherton Abbey. You know the meadow with the big rocks near Horseshoe Creek."

"Well, I've never heard it called Abbey something, but you know, we're into the monsoon season and you'd better consider the thunderstorms we're getting."

"We'll be leaving early enough to be back by noon. The rains don't usually start till afternoon."

That objection seemed to be settled, but Mr. Morgan decided to decline the invitation. "Mr. Thorpe and I will be going down to Santa Fe to do some research at a law firm there. I have reason to believe that I am able to claim an inheritance of considerable value, and I need to determine the proper procedure to lay claim to it according to New Mexico law." He smiled smugly and looked over at Christina and Jane. "My plans are to settle here in the Southwest, and I lack only a handsome piece of property and a charming woman to be my wife." I was told that the ladies of New Mexico are among the fairest, and I do agree that the examples before me have proven the rumor true."

Tommy and James chuckled and looked at the girls. Jane blushed, and Christina, who started to say something, choked on her enchilada, and began to cough. Her embarrassment was heightened by Tommy's concern as he jumped up and began pounding on her back.

After some sips of water, the coughing episode passed and Christina began to explain that she was only a guest and not a native of the Southwest, thereby hoping to exclude herself from Mr. Morgan's category of eligible brides. But James did not help. He suggested, "The Michigan girls are also among the most glamorous in our experience among the clientele here at the ranch."

The teasing banter went on through the main course, but in the interval between that and dessert Mr. Morgan leaned forward with his elbows on the table and the tips of his spread-apart fingers touching in a proprietary way as he enunciated very clearly with distinct words that drew his lips apart, revealing yellowed teeth, "I expect to acquire fortune enough to enable me to buy this very property."

Everyone was stunned. The young people did not know whether to laugh or stifle their smiles. Mr. Fairfax was too astonished to say, "But it's not for sale." James decided that this guest was the most obnoxious bragging prig he had ever seen.

And Mrs. Fairfax looked positively ill.

The long silence which followed Mr. Morgan's pronouncement showed that his words really had the desired effect, and he added slowly, "I am sure that any *sensible* young woman would be happy enough to accept an offer of marriage by the new owner of this estate."

The necessity of any reply was obviated by the crash of falling crockery and a scream from the kitchen. "Saca ese perro de aqui! (Get that dog out of here!) Has desperdecido mi postre! (You have ruined my dessert!) Estupido! Descarado! Inutil!"

They could hear José's voice. "Callate, Mujer! Me voy ahora." The ensuing scramble to see the destruction and oust the dog brought the dinner party to an end.

Chapter XIX

*There is a Time to wink as well
as to see.*

—Thomas Fuller

Jane knocked on the door to Christina's room at an early hour saying, "Let's go to Sotherton Abbey! Tommy will be getting the horses saddled up early. Breakfast in half an hour!"

Christina needed no second call. She had already dressed and was on her way downstairs five minutes later. Going through the den near the dining room, she interrupted what seemed to be a serious discussion between James and his parents. Their whispered conversation ceased as she entered and apologized. Mrs. Fairfax seemed agitated, but James turned to her with a smile saying, "It's a perfect day for the ride, but I'm sorry I can't go with you. I find that an urgent business matter takes me back to Santa Fe today. But next time, I'll be sure to go along. You need somebody besides Jane to protect you from Tommy's tricks."

"Jane has given me plenty of warning," laughed Christina. "I'm sure I'll be fine."

For a summer morning the air seemed crisp, but quite invigorating. Tommy helped her mount Brownie, the big gelding who seemed placid and friendly. Jane's horse was a beautiful gold color, and though eager to travel, stood quietly as Jane mounted. Tommy's copper colored quarterhorse, was named Hotshot because when asked, he could accelerate as though shot from a cannon. He led the way across the edge of the meadow, first on the road and then on a path into the pine forest.

Jane asked Christina if she had noticed the effects of altitude.

"I wondered why I was getting out of breath just coming downstairs this morning," Christina replied.

"Santa Fe is around seven thousand feet altitude and up here, we're a thousand feet higher. The cattle here are a special kind, bred to stand the high altitude because some cows can get brisket disease. And people often get headaches, or feel sleepy here, but I guess I'm used to it."

"I feel like I have to breathe faster," Christina said. "But I seem to have lots of energy. Maybe it's the excitement of being here. This is a beautiful place. I feel like I'm in a scene for a movie."

Delicado began to move faster, Brownie wanted to keep up, but his lumbering trot was a very uncomfortable gait for his inexperienced rider. The narrowing of the trail prevented further conversation as they proceeded single file, and as the trail became steeper, Christina was grateful that the horses were slowed to a walk.

The sun rose higher, and in spite of a breeze Christina began to feel hot and tired, but shortly after, she saw that Tommy had stopped up ahead by a little stream. They dismounted and the horses drank. The stream was fed by a sparkling spring that gushed down from about head height on the opposite side. Tommy invited the girls to jump across and drink. "This spring used to be just a trickle, hardly enough water to wet your fingers, but since the earthquake last year, it really pours out. Some deep rocks must've shifted and opened up a well."

After being assured that the water was potable ("It's from deep, deep, down in the earth– no cows down there."), Christina drank her fill.

Delicious and cool, it was most soothing. They re-filled their canteens and after a short rest resumed riding.

It seemed as if hours had passed, when Tommy reined in at the edge of a small meadow covered with boulders. "Here's Sotherton Abbey!" he announced and pointed at the rocks.

The meadow was backed by an almost vertical wall of rock, and the boulder-strewn expanse before it at first made no sense to Christina's eyes. It seemed to her that an immense giant must have stood on the rock wall and thrown down the rocks at random. Then Jane led her horse toward them and invited her to follow. Pointing at the first huge hunks, she said, "See how the rocks are in kind of a double circle? They say the ancient people used this as a sun and moon calendar. It's like an American Stonehenge!"

Tommy added, "See the big finger of rock atop the cliff wall? If you'd been here last winter at the solstice, you'd see how the rays of the rising sun cut through that opening and go right across that biggest rock here, to mark the day."

"Have you seen it?" Christina asked.

"It's too cold and too far away to get up here in December, so we just take the words of the scientists from the University that it happens."

"The religion of the early Indians really was tuned to the seasons, so I suppose you could consider this a religious place, even if it's not an actual abbey," conceded Christina.

"But you haven't seen the main attraction yet," Jane added.

"Come along downstream and see."

After a rather steep descent and a sharp turn around the edge of the vertical rock wall the stream cascaded in a series of little water-falls ending in a room-sized pool. Christina was amazed to see that steam was rising from the pool and more amazed that the pool was filled with a group of bathers! Seeing the riders approach-ing, the bathers, both men and women, yelled a greeting and emerged from the water, their naked bodies and long hair dripping as they scrambled out and stumbled away over the rocks laughing.

Tommy laughed at the look on Christina's face. She did not know what to say in her embar-rassment at seeing the naked bodies.

Jane seemed oblivious to the scene, prob-ably having encountered this situation before. And Christina realized that Jane and Tommy had been planning to show her this hot spring and were probably gratified that it could be visited when the shock value would be at its best.

"Gypsies." Jane explained. "They probably think we came to drive them out. It's our turn now to soak our feet." And she dismounted and began to take off her boots. Christina, relieved to know that she was not expected to disrobe completely, and still recovering from finding such revelers in this distant locale, did not voice the question in her mind: Did Jane and her brothers ever indulge in nude bathing here?

"Sit over here close to where the creek runs in. It's too hot on that side," Tommy suggested. "We didn't bring swim suits this time, but if you want to try the whole dip, we can come another time."

Christina enjoyed dangling her legs in the hot water, and wondered how she would explain her day in the letter she would write home that night. A prehistoric worship site, a hot spring pool with naked people, a horseback ride high into the mountains? Not only did it seem unbelievable, but maybe the entire episode had better not be mentioned, lest her mother disprove of her new friends and their unconventional entertainments.

They enjoyed the sandwiches Maria had packed for them, and laughed over the events of the previous evening. But all too soon Tommy declared the respite at an end as he saw the puffy cumulus clouds building over the mountaintop.

"It won't take us so long to get back," he explained. "We'll go down stream and get the forest road, instead of going back by the Abbey field."

But the descent seemed equally as long to Christina. Her legs were aching from the lurching movement of Brownie's broad back, and she could feel blisters rising on her calves just at the boot line. Imagine her surprise as they arrived at the forest road and saw James approaching in a rattling black pickup truck. He offered Christina a ride back with him in the truck, knowing the trip had probably been a little extreme for a guest unaccustomed to such a rigorous outing. She tried to demur politely at first, but on Jane and Tommy's urging, accepted gratefully.

"I was hoping I could get back from Santa Fe in time to rescue you," James explained. "Tommy always cuts out a little too much for first-timers."

"I'm glad too," Christina agreed. She felt like a heroine in distress who had been rescued by a true gentleman.

Chapter XX

*Everyone is a moon, and has
a dark side which he never shows
to anybody.*

—MARK TWAIN

Christina awoke sore and stiff, but resolved that her aches would not be evident to mar her gratitude for yesterday's adventures. She stretched and then rubbed her aching legs, dressed and descended the stairs with aplomb. Maria was serving breakfast for Mrs. Fairfax and the girls in the den, "To help them with their homework." But they all knew it was to avoid Mr. Morgan and Mr. Thorpe at the dining table. Mr. Fairfax said he could "brave the Brits" and although ready to counter any outrageous claims they made, he knew he was forced to use the diplomacy a host owes to paying guests. So he and his sons joined Mr. Morgan and Mr. Thorpe in the dining room for their beans, bacon, and green chile eggs served on a hot tortilla.

In spite of her main objective being the avoidance of obnoxious guests, Mrs. Fairfax was genuinely interested in the Austen class assignment. "An unmarried young lady going alone in a carriage with a man? Ay no! That was not to be heard of! It doesn't matter what kind of carriage. I think your teacher was trying to trick you."

"You're right!" Christina exclaimed. "The textbook describes all the various kinds of carriages, but we're also supposed to read Chapter Six, about courtship. And remember how in *Northanger Abbey*, Mr. Allen spoke against Catherine being driven in an open carriage with a man she was not related to?"

"Well, this will be an easy assignment then," laughed Jane. "All we need to do is to write down 'We wouldn't go at all' and hand in the paper."

Mrs. Fairfax demurred. "Yes, that's the correct answer, but after writing that, you'd better explain why and then tell the kind of carriage you'd have as a married lady."

As they finished their coffee and began writing, Mrs. Fairfax added, "I want to return to Santa

Fe early, so as soon as you finish, gather up your things to leave."

"Si, Mama, but I wanted to show Tina the Jemez Creek. Do we have to leave so soon?"

There was no reason given for her decided refusal, but the girls reluctantly complied.

Christina was disappointed also that she was taken back to Buttery Cottage instead of being invited to spend the rest of the afternoon and evening with Jane.

The week of classes began on a high note with the girls receiving good marks for their written essays on Carriages and Courtship. But for Christina the week ended with double distress.

Her first worry was about Jane's absence the latter part of the week. A phone call was answered with the excuse that her mother had taken her to Albuquerque to shop for a birthday dress. The up-coming party required much planning and the affair was to be quite grand with a hired hall and musicians. But after the second day, Jane's voice on the phone had a less cheerful tone. Christina wondered what the extra concern was about. Could she come and help? No, this was too deep a problem.

At dance class, Friday's session was to be, as much as possible, in costume, and Christina longed to see Jane's dress, but Jane did not appear. Tommy's unexpected appearance should have been a consolation, but even he seemed preoccupied and less charming. Christina had donned her one Regency gown, the yellow with black ribboned trim, and felt ready for the contra dances. Tommy had left his cowboy hat at home, tucked his pants into his socks in imitation of gentlemen's breeches, and wore a white silk scarf around his neck. "You look almost in style," Christina laughed.

He asked her for the first dance, and because he was concentrating on M. Solier's instructions during it, did not talk to her except once at the end of the set when he told her that Jane would like to see her that afternoon.

Christina happily acquiesced and looked forward to Tommy's second request to dance, during which she might discern the cause of the cloud that seemed to hang over the Fairfax family.

She could not refuse Ricardo's request to dance next, and although he seemed improved since her first struggling episode with him, he turned abruptly the wrong way during one maneuver, and because he kept hold of her hand, her arm was twisted back suddenly, causing a seam to tear in the back of her sleeve.

He apologized profusely, but because the tear was not noticeable, she said, "That's O.K. I should have let go of your hand. It's my fault." And they continued dancing, managing to complete the figure correctly to the satisfaction of both.

When M. Solier announced a ten-minute break, Christina took advantage of the time to repair her dress. She knew that Madame Solier would have in her green room needles and thread as well as pins for sartorial emergencies. She knocked only briefly, then opened the door, but what she saw caused her to stop in shock.

M. Solier was holding his wife's arm behind her, twisting it to cause her to writhe in pain and cry out. Their backs were to Christina, until her gasped "Oh!" caused him to turn around and see her in the doorway. Releasing Madame Solier immediately, he frowned and growled, "Get out! This is a private dressing room."

Christina wasted no time in backing out and closing the door, but then stood in an amazed stupor, unable to move. Suddenly, the door opened again and Madame stood before her, crying softly.

"Please, forgive me. I am all right. He sometimes loses patience with me. He is so short tempered. Please say nothing of this, I beg you. Promise me you will tell no one. Please."

"But,...don't..."

"No, no. I cannot answer your questions now. Please say I am busy. You must go back to the hall. But I beg you again, say nothing of this. Will you please agree?"

"Yes," Christina mumbled as she backed away slowly. In a daze, she went first to the drinking fountain and stood in line behind other thirsty dancers, then went through the first open door next to the hall, an empty classroom where she could sit down and control her shaking disbelief. But it was there she received her second shock. Tommy and Mary Sidney were embracing behind the door!

They jumped apart as soon as Christina entered, and all three young people stood for a few seconds staring at each other. Then Tommy said, "Excuse me. It's time to get back to the dance." And he left ahead of Mary, who followed him at a distance. But as she passed Christina, Mary turned and smiled at her.

Chapter XXI

The heart is forever
inexperienced.

—HENRY DAVID THOREAU

Christina was doubly devastated. Her intended hero was not hers after all. And a married couple, who she thought were perfectly suited to each other, were discovered to be in a most painful relationship. How deceiving appearances can be!

She berated herself for believing Tommy was to be her sweetheart. But had not Jane encouraged the friendship by suggesting she and Tommy were meant for each other? Jane had warned her that Tommy was a charmer and a flirt, but even if the embrace behind the door was a momentary indiscretion, his choice brought a stab of jealousy to Christina's heart. She could no longer be a friend to Mary Sidney.

Even though reason would force her to admit that not all marriages could be perfect, Christina had never known an unsuitable match. Divorce was unknown in her family and among their acquaintances. Were there other husbands who were secretly torturing their wives? She shuddered at the thought and her world suddenly seemed to grow darker.

She longed for the consolation of friendship and hastened to visit Jane as soon as classes ended for the day. She rang the bell at the gate, but when Maria opened it, she saw from the look on the maid's face that the cloud was hanging over the entire Fairfax household. Jane met her in the foyer and without a greeting led her to her bedroom where she turned and faced Christina with the news, "I found out that I'm adopted!"

"What? How do you know?"

"My mother told me. But now I must say my adoptive mother."

"Do you know who your real mother is?"

"She's Aunt Phyllida!"

"Who is your real father?"

"My mom says he was killed in the war."

"Why didn't your parents tell you sooner?"

"There's a problem about my inheritance. The title was not clear and Mom was told to conceal my real identity. I am to receive a large amount of money on my eighteenth birthday, but Mom had to tell me sooner, because of that man, that Cecil Morgan."

"You mean that obnoxious guest who's looking for a wife?

I can't believe all this! You look just like your dad and Tommy. Is that man related to you?"

"Yes, he's actually my cousin. Oh, Tina, isn't this terrible!"

And here she began to cry. The two girls stood in an embrace while Christina patted Jane's back and tried to offer some comforting words. Her own distress now seemed minor by comparison.

Chapter XXII

*Today's misery is tomorrow's
novel.*

—IVAN ASHROTH

Mrs. Fairfax entered with coffee and cookies. She was pleased to see Christina, and realizing that Christina would be a comfort to Jane, asked her to stay the weekend. Christina kept expressing her disbelief that the Englishman could be a relative, and Mrs. Fairfax reiterated, "He may be a relative, but he is definitely not a part of this family! Jane will always be my loving daughter, and no matter how hard he tries, he cannot have her inheritance."

"Is that why they're going to the lawyers in Santa Fe?"

"Cecil has discovered that Phyllida died here and is trying to lay claim to her estate."

"But what right has he to do that?"

"Old Mr. Morgan's will follows the ancient English law of primogeniture. That means the inheritance is through the males of the family only, and Cecil is Phyllida's closest male relative."

"That's terrible! It's just like the Bennet family in *Pride and Prejudice* with silly Mr. Collins due to inherit Longbourn. But that was eighteenth century England, and this is twentieth century America. That law cannot be enforced here, can it?"

"James and Mr. Fairfax are consulting with our lawyer, and I'm sure they'll be able to enforce justice. And before she died, Phyllida entrusted all her research to the archives of the State Library here. James is applying to access her papers, hoping to find something that applies to her case."

"It all sounds so unbelievable. It's like we're living in a storybook. Cecil Morgan is the villain, and fat Mr. Thorpe is his accomplice."

Here Jane began to smile and enter into the conversation.

"Someday we can write all this in a book. It will be a best selling story of crime and punishment."

"Yes," added Christina, "and we'll double your fortune by selling the story to the movies. But they'll probably tinker with it so much it won't be anything like the book!"

Mrs. Fairfax said, "I'll tell you more of what Phyllida told me of her family and about her escape to this country. You will think it's stranger than a fairy tale."

"Tell us," cried Christina. "We'll write it down." And they settled back with their cookies to munch and listen. Afterward, they embellished the story with fabricated details, laughing as they wrote and thereby lessening their own discomfiture.

A True Fairy Tale
By Jane and Christina

Once, many years ago, there lived in England a baronet named Sir Ronald Kempton Morgan. Because his father Sir William Eliott Morgan, of Kellynch Hall had been a spendthrift, having eventually to rent out his manor house and live in a cheap apartment in Bath, Sir Ronald learned from that bad example. He took up thrifty habits and a frugal lifestyle, recouped his father's losses, invested wisely, diversified his portfolio, expanded his estate, and amassed a tidy fortune. He closed off most of the rooms in the manor in order to save heat and electricity, kept only two servants and drove an older model car that he kept as finely tuned as he did his guitar.

His good wife Lady Helen, supporting his thrifty lifestyle, made all his shirts and darned his socks, and entertained guests for dinner only when money-saving coupons for groceries were available.

But they spared no expense for the education of their only daughter, little Phyllida, a beautiful and intelligent child. They hired private tutors for her for each separate subject. Señora Margaret from Spain instructed her in Spanish, Madame Krohn in mathematics, Mr. Ixie in dancing, Virginia Swineott in cards and etiquette, and Jacqueline Quarbushel in painting and needlework.

Sir Ronald borrowed books for her from the library at Pemberley, which was the work of many generations, and Phyllida, became so well read, she took to wearing blue stockings and doing scholarly research.

Her mother, Lady Helen, had only one worry. According to the laws of primogeniture, Sir Ronald's estate was bequeathed to the nearest male descendant, not daughter Phyllida. A cousin, Cecil Morgan of Longbourn, was to be the heir. Sir Ronald had it in his power to change the rule of succession, and Lady Helen urged him to do so, but he responded to her constant reminders, only with, "Yeah, yeah, I'm getting around to it," and put off the paper work in the press of more immediate concerns, including the many requests to play his guitar at neighborhood festivities.

One day at Lexicon cards with her friends Mrs. Berryhack, and Mrs. Myra, Lady Helen played the word GATE, and as Mrs. Berryhack played the word GOOD to connect with it, she said, "That reminds me that Anne Brandengate is a good financial advisor and seer. Sir Ronald would do well to get her advice." And Lady Helen quickly made an appointment for Sir Ronald to see her.

Mrs. Brandengate looked into her *Wall Street Journal,* her financial tables, and into her crystal ball, and gave this advice to Sir Ronald: A war is imminent. Put your holdings into gold and get it out of the country. Sir Ronald believed and complied.

Because gold is very heavy and difficult to transfer discreetly, he devised an ingenious plan. He made a series of transAtlantic crossings on the Cunard Line ships with tiny bars of gold concealed in hollow books, and gold coins in the heels of his shoes.

In America he traveled by train, and deposited the gold, bit by bit, in rented safety deposit boxes in banks all across the West, emptying his shoes first, then the books. (The heavy suitcases were a good workout for his shoulder muscles, but the coins in his shoes required higher heels and made for awkward walking.) Then he gave his daughter the tiny keys to each box on a necklace of gold.

When Cecil Morgan came of age, two things became clear to him. The first was that he was very averse to earning his own living, and the second was that he believed he was entitled to his Uncle Ronald's estate when Uncle Ronald died. He began to dream of little schemes for hastening Sir Ronald's death, but they proved unnecessary when Sir Ronald was found dead of a heart attack one morning, slumped over the Lexicon table with the letters PHYLLIDA spelled out in cards before him.

Lady Helen made it clear to Cecil that all her husband's assets had gone to Phyllida, and he needed to go seek employment for himself instead of searching for inherited wealth. Phyllida had by this time emigrated to America to study at Yale, and to do research in the summers at various universities in the West.

Cecil took a series of menial jobs, trying to earn money to search for Phyllida. When he heard she had gone to America, he secured passage on the *SS Ryndam* by becoming a dance instructor and partner for the single old ladies who had no escorts. He became friends with another male escort named Thorpe, who had been dropped from law studies at Oxford but still considered himself a qualified solicitor.

Here the "True Fairy Tale" must be truncated to allow for present events to unfold, and to allow Mrs. Fairfax to relate the continued story of Phyllida in a more serious and factual style.

Chapter XXIII

*Let me not to the marriage of true
minds admit impediments.*

—William Shakespeare

The Story of Phyllida
By Lola Fairfax

I am telling my daughter Jane about her birth mother. We have talked many hours since I have revealed that Edward and I have adopted her, and she asks that I write down how it all happened.

We first met Phyllida when she came here as a summer guest. She had been visiting guest ranches in many states in the summers and teaching seminars in different colleges during the winters. I sensed that there was something wrong, when she asked me not to put her name on a guest list or tell any phone caller that she had been here. I thought she was running away from a cruel husband, and I did not ask her about it.

We became friends almost instantly. I admired her spirit and her intelligence. She loved my little boys, the ranch, and our rides together over the Caldera meadow. She said she thought I had the perfect life, and I remember saying it is perfect except for one thing—I had so much wanted a daughter. I love my boys, but I was unable to have any more children.

She returned every summer after that and we became even closer friends. On Maria's day off we experimented with her recipes and enjoyed cooking for Edward and the boys. Then one summer she came back for only three days, saying that she may not return for a long time because she would be the entire summer at a Michigan seminar and hoped to gain a permanent teaching job there for the school year.

But a month later she was back with the news that she was married! She had met the ideal man, she said. It was a whirlwind romance, but they knew they were ideally suited—both from England, both in academic careers, and with the same ideals and beliefs. They would take their honeymoon here at the ranch, but he had already enlisted with the British army to fight in the war. At that time, Germany was sending bombers over England, and the United States was not yet involved. With no time to buy proper rings or have them sized to fit, they bought little-finger rings at the nearest jewelers and were married in an Episcopal chapel.

She taught at a Michigan college for the first semester only, then returned here to the ranch. I could see she was expecting a child. But she looked weak and sick. I thought it was due to the worry about her husband. I knew his first name was William, but she never told me his last name. He had no family and had listed the Fairfax family as next of kin. Phyllida was still afraid of whoever was pursuing her and feared he would find her, so she kept her identity concealed.

Then came the terrible telegram that William was missing in action. Our grief was so great, but our prayers were greater, until the day a package arrived with his dog tag identification and the message, "Declared dead."

The only thing that kept her from complete despair was the expectation of the baby. Her lying-in went well, and Maria brought a curandera to attend the birth, even though we wanted to take her to the hospital in Santa Fe. What joy to see that the little one was delivered safely and that she was healthy. Our beautiful little Jane!

But Phyllida was not healthy. She knew that a spot on her breast had turned inward, and the poisonous cancer had spread through her body. We took her to the hospital, but the doctors could do no more than soften her pain and declared that she had only a few months to live. Edward and I had already agreed to be godparents, and now we promised to raise Jane as our own. Phyllida signed the papers making the adoption legal, and gave us the gold necklace with all the little keys. We promised to give them to Jane on her eighteenth birthday. The necklace, along with the little wedding ring and other jewelry, was secured in the safe deposit bank in the closest town, Los Alamos. Jane shall have them on her birthday.

Chapter XXIV

Little secrets are commonly told again, but great ones generally kept.

—Lord Chesterfield

While Jane was learning the history of her birth mother, and Christina digesting it with her, James and Mr. Fairfax were searching Phyllida's archives for information to use in the defense of the inheritance. James had brought a large box of manuscripts, books, and articles, for his mother to peruse.

"But there should be more," Lola protested. "I'm sure she kept a diary. And she must have sent it with these things to the library."

"There was a fire in one of the upper floors about five years ago," James replied. "I remember some books were removed from the archive floor because of the possibility of water damage. I'll check with their office again to see if they were returned here, or where they would be now."

Another concern for the family was the preparation for the birthday party. A hall had been rented in Santa Fe a year in advance, but it was now unavailable because the kitchen had been declared below code. Repairs would not be completed for many months. A search was made for other venues but all were either too distant, too small, or too shabby to meet the family's requirements.

"What about the barn?" Tommy asked. "The horses could be stabled in the shed or in the corrals while we're fixing it up."

"You can't have a dance on an uneven dirt floor," James said.

José put in his advice. "We've got time to level it and have concrete poured, haven't we?"

Mr. Fairfax demurred. "There's nothing worse than dancing on old hard cement. But a wooden floor atop of that would work.

Big bucks, but what the hell! Even if she loses her money, Jane deserves a big bash. Lola has been worried about the size of the guest list. Well, let's go for it. This will be a party the whole county will remember."

And so the work was begun. Contractors were secured, lumber ordered, renovation plans were drawn, and extra workmen hired. And the guest list grew to an amazing length: classmates and friends, neighbors and relatives, the Rho Sigma boys and all of Buttery Cottage, including Mrs. Buttery herself. Dr. Roy, the Austen class instructor would come, and even Dr. Barber was not to be cut from the list! Santa Fe Trail buffs and Austen Society clubs were contacted. Jane declared the party would be a costume ball, a combination of Old West and Regency England, and guests could dress in either of those styles.

During this time, Christina was living entirely with the Fairfax family. "I have gained an extra mom," Jane declared, "but even though I have lost her, I think that I have gained a sister. Stay here, Tina, and help me plan the party. I want your family to come from Michigan also."

"Oh, what an idea!" Christina laughed. "Lilly will be so excited. And my folks will have to come because they would never let Lilly come by herself on the train. I hope Mr. Saxon is well enough to come. They did say in the last letter that he was coming to Santa Fe soon."

Then during one late-night planning session in Jane's bedroom, the girls exchanged two secrets. Jane broached the session by mentioning

Tommy's dancing and his telling her what a good time he'd had at the dance class. "Except for one thing," Jane added. "That minx Mary Sidney embarrassed him to death. You probably didn't know how she tricked him. She told him to come see a cartoon of himself that someone had put on the blackboard in the math classroom. He followed her to see and when they were behind the door, she kissed him!"

Christina did not reveal that she had witnessed that encounter herself, nor that Tommy seemed to be a willing participant. "Did he enjoy it?" she asked.

"He was probably flattered, but more embarrassed than anything. I think he prefers you over all the girls, but she's after him. She's so bold."

"I don't think I could ever lure a boy that way," Christina said. "But now I have a secret to tell you."

And she related the incident of the torn sleeve, her dash to the Solier green room, and the discovery of the painful situation she had witnessed there.

Jane was appalled. "Are you sure? How terrible! Do you think it was a one-time incident?"

"Do you remember our remarking about the unusual birthmark on Madame Solier's chin? Have you noticed that it has gone away? I think it was a bruise, not a birthmark. I think he beats her in private!"

"Horrible man! What can we do? We have invited them to direct the Austen dances at the party. How can we stop his cruelty?"

"She made me promise that I would say nothing!"

Here, Mrs. Fairfax entered the bedroom and, reminding them how late the hour was, suggested that Christina return to her own room and continue their gossip session the next day at the ranch.

"Will Cecil Morgan be there?" Jane asked.

"He and Mr. Thorpe have gone to another lawyer in Albuquerque," Mrs. Fairfax replied. "We'll have the ranch to ourselves."

Chapter XXV

The next day at the ranch Christina came upon Jane in her room going over items from a small velvet bag. "These are some pieces of my mother's jewelry. Mom decided to give them to me now, rather than wait till my birthday."

She held up a tiny gold ring. "Look at this ring. This must be the little-finger ring they bought for a wedding ring." She held it up for Christina to see. "I can't put it on my left hand because my little finger is bent—kind of webbed. Had you noticed? But it fits on my right hand."

Christina stood as if struck by lightning. Memories whirled in her head. Where had she seen that ring before? The edges were delicately scalloped. And where had she seen a left hand with the little finger curiously bent like that? Mr. Saxon's hand! For some moments she could hardly speak. What a strange coincidence! Then she said, "Jane, did you find your father's last name on any jewelry or on his identification tag?"

"No, but here are some initials on this cross." And she held up a silver cross on a chain, much tarnished but inscribed on the back with a heart and the legible initials W. A. S.

"W. Saxon? Could it be the same name as my teacher? Maybe he was the brother of your real father! Let's look at the I.D. tag." And they rushed to her mother's room to open the little box of mementoes. Finding the tag, they examined it under the light, but the metal tag was bent and the writing obscured. The name could be Saxon or Sutton or Samson. It was impossible to tell for sure.

"I'll call my dad and ask him to find out if Mr. Saxon had a brother in the war. Wouldn't it be exciting to discover another relative? Maybe you have an uncle in Michigan!"

"My mother said he had no family. But it doesn't hurt to ask."

Christina's mind was whirling with further possibilities, but not wanting to mention the shape of the ring and Mr. Saxon's fingers and lead Jane into speculation with possible disappointment, she said no more.

All through breakfast thoughts crowded her mind and made her appear distracted. What if Jane's father had not been killed in the war? What if the report of his death were a horrible mistake?

What if Mr. Saxon had searched for Phyllida and had been unable to find her on returning from Europe? What if he did not know he had a daughter?

"You look tired, Tina. You don't have to go to church with us. I got you girls up so early because we like the early service at the Chili Line Church. Father Kelly always gives such good sermons."

"I'm O.K. But I am rather tired. Maybe I'll go back to bed and later get some history done."

But as soon as the house was empty Christina went to the second floor storage room, where she hoped James had put the extra papers about Phyllida that he had found in the archives.

Luckily, the door was unlocked. She went in quietly, and the first thing she spotted was a huge old book. The leather-looking cover was imprinted with illegible gold characters. She lifted the cover and jumped back in alarm when she heard cackling laughter and a high voice warning "Forbidden! Forbidden!" She quickly closed the cover and turned to see James standing in the doorway laughing.

"You've discovered Tommy's old Halloween book. I'm surprised the batteries are still good enough to make the witch talk."

But Christina was chagrined. She was caught snooping in her hosts' private papers! "I wanted to see the top of the Family Tree that Jane had showed me downstairs. I'm so sorry. I thought everyone had gone to church. That is, I...." Everything she said seemed to enforce her guilt and embarrassment. Seeing the tears in her eyes, James put his arm around her, and said, "Don't worry. That's O.K. You don't need to feel so bad." But his comforting words only increased her distress. And she found herself telling him of the real object of her search. He took her hand gently, and listened to her idea. He did not laugh or deny its possibility. He became more interested when she mentioned the ring, and the initials on the cross. "A webbed pinkie finger is an inherited trait," he said. "Let's look for more evidence. We need to call the War Office or the British records office. Maybe we can find his real name by the number on the tag. As I recall, the number was legible enough, wasn't it?"

"And I need to call home and find Mr. Saxon's first and middle names. The telegram he sent me on the train was signed W. Saxon. That fits with the W.A.S. on the cross!"

They decided not to reveal their suspicions to Jane or to the rest of the family until they had more information. Christina was most gratified to find that James had listened to her with sympathy.

Chapter XXVI

*Against the assault of laughter
nothing can stand.*

—MARK TWAIN

While the barn renovation was in progress, Mrs. Fairfax, Jane, and Christina were assiduously attending to the thousand decisions required for a celebration of such a magnitude that it seemed almost overwhelming. Decorations and fixtures for the barn in order to transform it into a ballroom were the first concern. "This will be no barn dance," Mr. Fairfax had declared. He ordered James and Tommy to bring him pictures of magnificent ballrooms and palatial dancing halls.

Tommy reminded him, "Remember, Dad, it's supposed to be part Western. Not everyone likes or even knows about old England. Jane wants everyone to be comfortable."

"Well, should we have silk settees on one side and baled hay seats on the other side of the room?"

"Ask Jane."

"Her mother will make the final decisions. I'm dealing with the wiring and plumbing. Take these pictures to her and let me out of the ruffles and furbelows."

Of no minor concern for the ladies was the choice of gowns for the ball. Christina quoted from *Mansfield Park*: "A woman can never be too fine while she is all in white. I think you should wear a white gown with gold trim, Jane."

"We can be sisters, both in white."

"Oh, no. You are the birthday person, the honoree. I prefer a pale blue. With lavender trim."

Shopping in Santa Fe and Albuquerque produced no ball gowns of Regency style; therefore dressmakers were required. There followed the continual sound of sewing machines, and the mumbling of women with pins in their mouths while they made adjustments in front of tall mirrors. There was the constant ring of the telephone, and tradesmen knocking on the gate to deliver boxes.

At the ranch, trucks came and went, the sound of hammers and drills filled the air, and the horses snorted in startled annoyance at the disruptions. It was a matter of wonder to the men that their two unwelcome guests remained lodged there and stood watching the construction with curiosity.

With Maria in town tending to the preparations with the girls, only José was left to perform the culinary duties for the men of the family and the crew of carpenters at the ranch. His menus relied heavily on beans and tortillas, but the men knew that any complaints would result in requests for help, and their hunger after a session of hard work produced the appetites that declared no pickles were required.

One evening, seated across from Mr. Fairfax at one end of a long table filled with the crew, Cecil Morgan made a startling statement. "I have discovered that Phyllida Morgan actually lived here and has left her large fortune to Jane. To avoid further litigation and claims on the property, I am suggesting that an arrangement can be made which will satisfy everyone. Therefore, I am requesting the hand of your daughter Jane in marriage."

On hearing that outrageous proposal, Mr. Fairfax choked on his bean soup and coughed a mouthful of it out onto the table.

José began to laugh. James began to chuckle, Tommy positively guffawed, and the other diners, some not even hearing the joke, joined in until the entire table was an uproar of laughter.

Cecil turned red with consternation. His lower lip trembled as if he were trying to say something more, but the noise of ridicule overwhelmed him and he got up and left the table with Mr. Thorpe following. After things had calmed down a bit and Mr. Fairfax had recovered his breath, he followed the two men out onto the porch and asked in a calm voice, "Did you two gentlemen wish to check out of your lodgings here?"

"Are you telling us to leave? That will add to the evidence in our case against you."

"Certainly not, Guys. We can put up with you, as long you keep paying your bill, and we can sure use the extra fun at the dinner table!"

Mr. Cecil Morgan and Mr. Thorpe turned, descended the porch steps, and walked toward their cabin without saying a word more.

Chapter XXVII

*He loved the twilight that
surrounds The border-land of old
romance.*

—HENRY WADSWORTH LONGFELLOW

William Albert Saxon was packing his valise
in preparation for a trip west, as he had done so
many times in years past. But on this occasion,
his spirits were soaring in anticipation of finally
finding the information that had so long eluded
him.

He looked up at the mantelpiece where the
tiny photo portrait of his wife sat, picked it up,
sighed deeply and put it into the suitcase. He recalled her tearful goodbye and his promise to return from the war for a proper honeymoon, but
it was not to be.

He wanted to forget the months and years that followed that goodbye; the terrible pain and confusion of the battlefield, the agony of seeing comrades die beside him, the wound that festered and caused him to lose his leg, the horrors of the German concentration camp, and the failed escape attempt. The image that sustained him through it all was the face of his beautiful bride. He had promised her that he would return, and a vision of her appeared before him every evening, no matter where he was.

Until, one night he awoke with a start thinking he had heard her cry out to him. He sat up for a long time, unable to sleep, and suddenly realized the vision of her face had vanished. She had died. He did not know how he knew, but he knew.

After the end of the war, his release from the enemy camp, and many months of hospitalization and surgeries, he returned to America to find her. Her last letter had come from Michigan where they had met, but he could not trace her there. Remembering some of the western states she had mentioned, he researched the names of guest ranches and bed-and-breakfast inns and called them, asking each if her name had been on their register. Some gave quick negative replies concerning only the current year. A few did look in files of past years, trying to locate her name, but there were no listings for a Phyllida Saxon. He recalled also her explanation to him of her fear of a cousin who may be pursuing her with evil intentions; thus, he surmised she possibly had used a pseudonym in most of her hotels.

The likeliest possibility was the Fairfax Ranch in New Mexico. He remembered her mention of the name of Lola Fairfax as a special friend there, but all calls resulted in negative answers. Each summer he traveled to a different western state for a guest ranch vacation, hoping to learn of her through a wild coincidence, a chance remark at the breakfast table, or a description of her as a beautiful and memorable woman.

He began repeating the calls each spring when he knew the summer hostelries would be open-ing. This spring, a call to the Fairfax Ranch gave him his first information.

The phone was answered by a man named José, probably one of the ranch hands. "She came here a long time ago, but she died," he said.

William Saxon gasped and began asking, "When? How?"

But the man hung up the phone immediately. Trying again, he received a different person with the same negative answer. "We have never had anyone here by that name."

But that one "José call" gave him the only incentive he needed to travel to New Mexico. He planned to teach at the Regency Seminar in Santa Fe and use the weekends to stay at the ranch and perhaps learn more about his lost love. Then came the sudden illness on the train and his recuperation, until he received a call from his student Christina with the most startling information. "Yes, he would come. A big party for a Jane Fairfax? *Possible information about a relative*? Dress in Regency style? Yes, Yes, and No, he would not need transportation from Lamy Station. Thank you so much, Tina. I'll see you soon."

Chapter XXVIII

Violence is the last refuge of the incompetent.

—Isaac Asimov

The barn renovation was almost complete. Most of the extra workers had already left, but Mr. Fairfax, James, Tommy, and José, with three neighbor men, were adding the final touches. Earlier in the day they had placed the settees, benches, and chairs for the Regency guests, and now were unloading bales of hay from a truck. The bales, covered with horse blankets, would serve as benches for the cowboy set, and would be used later to feed the horses.

Cecil and Thorpe had just returned from Albuquerque with new ammunition for their upcoming lawsuit, and eager to present their findings to the Fairfax men, headed toward the barn to talk with them.

"Grab a bale," said Tommy. "We're storing the extra bales against the wall to serve as a buffet table."

But Cecil and his friend merely stood watching, till Mr. Fairfax asked, "What now? I suppose that paper you're holding is some medieval legal document saying we owe you some money?"

Mr. Thorpe straightened his corpulent body to an authoritative pose and spoke loudly. "We have completed our conference with our legal advisors, and although you say that Phyllida's daughter is to inherit her estate, there is no proof that she is a legitimate heir. Bastards cannot be named as successors."

José was closest to them, and turned saying angrily, "Who're you calling a bastard, you sonnabeech? Get outta here!" and landed a blow to Thorpe's chin.

Thorpe pushed José with a thrust that sent him to the ground, and before he could rise, Tommy was hitting Thorpe, with Cecil trying to intervene.

Mr. Fairfax and James attempted to separate the combatants, but the three neighbor men jumped into the fray, and with José now adding more insults and blows, the scene became a tangled melee, a dog-and-cat fight of major proportions.

Suddenly, a large stream of water from a hose hit José, and then Thorpe in the face, and a deep voice called out, "Gentlemen! Gentlemen! What is this riot? Cease immediately! You should be ashamed for resorting to violence. Let us discuss your differences calmly and rationally."

The dampened fighters paused and saw a tall, gray-haired man with a cane, the water hose in his other hand. He shut off the water and said, "Let me introduce myself. I am William Saxon, husband of the late Phyllida Morgan Saxon and father of Jane Saxon Fairfax."

The dampened men stared in amazement. Mr. Fairfax brushed himself off and came forward, extending his hand. "Our apologies, Sir. This is not our usual method of discussion. Welcome to Fairfax Ranch."

****

William Saxon had phoned ahead for a rental car to meet him at Lamy, and following the directions of the driver with the address Christina had given him, found his way to the Santa Fe house, where the women were waiting anxiously. One can only imagine the emotions felt at the meeting of father and daughter.

William was almost overcome at seeing Jane. For him, it was as if his Phyllida were revived in her person before him. Jane embraced her father, then laughed and took his hand with the ring, showing its duplicate on her own right hand.

There would be time later for explanations, reminiscences, and getting acquainted, but for now, there was a rush to get to the ranch by the dinner hour and meet the rest of the family. William marveled at the timing of his arrival there and laughed at reprising his role as a teacher having to halt a schoolboy fight.

Chapter XXIX

*If pleasures are greatest in
anticipation, just remember that
this is also true of trouble.*

—ELBERT HUBBARD

Jane and Christina were in Jane's room happily discussing the final arrangements for the party. "I'm so glad your family can come," Jane said. "I'm looking forward to meeting your sister Lilly."

"She is beside herself with excitement. She wants to see the little rings and meet your new real dad. She had seen him in the halls at school, but had no idea that he would be a part of our whole story."

"What a coincidence, the way we found him. If this were a novel, it would be criticized for having a contrived plot."

"Lots of novels are filled with coincidence. That's because they happen in real life. Truth is stranger than fiction."

"I'm so glad James found my mother's extra papers and her diaries in the other library. They really proved my parents were married and made me a legitimate child."

"For sure! That defeated Cecil and Thorpe for good. They can't have any grounds for claiming your inheritance now. But I wonder why they're still hanging around. I don't trust them."

"Well, for one thing it's the food. Didn't you notice what gluttons they are? Where else can they get meals like Maria and Mom fix? And I think they want to come to the party. Remember that they were male escorts on the ships, and I'll bet they think they can charm some rich old ranch widows with their dancing."

Both girls laughed at the thought. They recalled the men walking away from the barn in their wet clothes. "I wish we'd been there five minutes earlier to see Mr. Saxon give them that dousing," Christina added. "Mr. Saxon is so great. Your mom says you and he will open the ball as partners in the Grand March. I can hardly wait."

"And I'll bet Tommy will ask you to march right behind us. Has he asked you?"

Christina answered in the negative, and secretly hoped that James would ask her. Their long connivance in the solution of the family mystery, his kind attentiveness to her ideas, his rescuing her on the day of the long ride from the hot spring: all had impressed her, and were beginning to turn her heart toward him. She was beginning to prefer dark Spanish-looking men over blond, curly-headed ones.

The morning before the big event was sunny with the traditional New Mexico blue skies, but in the afternoon the puffy cumulus turned to dark overcast and the mountain monsoon rained down in force. Then it cleared suddenly, leaving everything sparkling in the late afternoon sun. This was a typical summer pattern for the high mountains of the state, but knowing how the storms could sometimes prove severe with washed out roads, many of the guests arrived early and planned to stay the entire weekend, guaranteeing not only that they could dance till dawn, but also drive home in the daylight after an extra day's rest. So the little guest cabins were filling up. An ox roast, and a bean-and-pig pit were in progress, and the "bale buffet" was being loaded with refreshments.

Two groups of musicians, Gus and His Western Rattlers and the Queen's Chamber Music, were setting up at the head of the hall. They agreed that by alternating their programs, they would be able to play to a much later hour. Gus would call the square and round dances, and Monsieur Solier would direct the English contra dances.

The arrangements augured well for a perfect evening, with only a more-severe-than-usual weather forecast, and the problem of moving the piano down to the barn. But our partygoers could not know that the night would be much different from expected.

Chapter XXX

On with the dance! Let joy be unconfined; No sleep till morn, when Youth and Pleasure meet, to chase the glowing hours with flying feet.

—Lord Byron

For the Grand March opening of the ball the two musical groups played together, and the order of march had been carefully planned by Mrs. Fairfax. At the head marched Mr. Saxon and his newly discovered daughter Jane, the birthday honoree. Mr. Saxon was attired in a gray coat and knee breeches with matching stockings and black dancing slippers. So well did he manage his prosthesis, without limping, that the cane seemed only a decorative accessory.

Jane was resplendent in a white empire style gown trimmed with gold ribbon. Her long white gloves reached almost to the short sleeves of the dress whose low neckline showed off her pearl necklace and the matching pearl tiara encircling her blonde curls.

Next were Mr. and Mrs. Fairfax, she in Spanish lace with a black shawl and mantilla, he in a tan western suit with leather boots and matching vest.

Behind them came the Dashwoods. Mrs. Dashwood, understanding a little of the dual nature of the theme of the ball, had chosen a pale green, long silk dress with low-cut neckline.

Mr. Dashwood, not quite approving of his wife's décolletage, yet wanting to appear "western" in a proper way, wore, on the advice of Mr. Saxon, a pair of Levi's with a suit jacket.

Next came our heroine in pale blue, looking older with her brown hair arranged high in curls with dark blue ribbons. She was secretly thrilled to have James as her partner instead of Tommy, even though she thought that arrangement had been chosen by Mrs. Fairfax. "My oldest son should be the next in line," she had said.

Tommy, as her second son, was happy to honor Christina's little sister Lilly as escort. With her braids wrapped around her head, and her frilly pink dress, Lilly resembled a dancing musical doll. She could hardly keep from skipping with excitement.

Next were Maria and José, followed by a long line of neighbors and relatives, classmates and teachers, as well as friends from as near as Santa Fe, and as far away as London. They marched the length of the hall, divided and came down again as couples, repeated as lines of four, then eight, then divided again into a single line that circled in upon itself with laughter, pulling, and jostling.

When the line was restored to couples, Monsieur Solier divided the line into sixes, and as the Queen's Chamber musicians took over, he directed the dancers in a lively contra dance that resulted in each couple progressing down the length of the entire hall, while their counterparts were traveling in the opposite direction.

After a pause, the students from the dance class demonstrated the minuet. As Christina and James took the mincing steps and bowed, James said, "I intend to ask you for the dance after this one also."

"But that would be improper," Christina smiled. "Regency etiquette does not allow more than two dances together for couples who are not engaged."

"You are counting the Grand March ending as the first dance? Then you are correct. I requested that you be my partner, even before my mother set up the order of march! And shall we add to the scandal by sitting down together after that?"

"Very well," Christina replied, laughing.

The next set was the western squares, and because the majority of dancers were familiar with the calls, the rhythm was accelerated to an exhausting pace. As it ended, James led Christina to a chair, but as soon as she was seated, Tommy approached, grabbed her hand, and swung her into a polka. He paid no attention to her protests that she was already promised for this one. But as they finished the first circuit of the floor, James tapped his shoulder. "May I cut in?" and not waiting for an answer, led Christina to the door outside. She was grateful to catch her breath in the cool air with time to marvel at the scene before her.

The sky was wide enough to present several different scenarios at once. Towering cumulus were building on one side, next to curtains of dark virgas, which threatened to drop their moisture and become sheets of rain. Ragged cirrus clouds were moving to the east, reflecting an orange sunset on their lower edges. Then, a tiny zigzag of lightning in the distance illuminated the darkest bank of clouds, followed by the faint rumble of thunder.

"Tommy must have left the corral gate open," James said. "The other horses are in the stable, but I see Hotshot is way out in the meadow. I'll tell him. But it's no problem. He comes when Tommy calls to him. Let's go back inside. I have an idea. Let's climb up to the hayloft where we can have a view of the dance floor."

Christina agreed. "It's almost as much fun to watch as to dance." She felt also that James was trying to prevent her from dancing again with Tommy, and she was secretly gratified at the thought. What young girl could help being pleased at being the focus of such a brotherly rivalry. Climbing the ladder to the loft in a dark corner was difficult in her long dress, but the view from the edge was great entertainment. There was short Dr. Barber steering Mrs. Buttery around the floor in a surprisingly smooth dance, giving the impression of a tugboat controlling an ocean liner. Maria was laughing at her husband José who seemed to make more progress vertically than horizontally as he jumped with each step, even when the music called for a glide. Two small children were seriously, as if counting, taking two steps to the side and two back, with stiff knees and huge strides. Danielle, in a bright red

dress, was dancing with Ricardo, and doing quite
well. Christina surmised that Danielle was the
one leading. She was most pleased at the sight of
her mother and father dancing expertly around
the floor. Because her father had always worked
the evening shift, her parents had seldom gone
dancing as far as Christina could remember. Now
she was proud of their dancing and pleased that
they enjoyed it.

Soon there was the demonstration of the scandalous waltz by Monsieur and Madame Solier.
Madame's full skirts billowed around her as she
and her partner gave the impression of flying,
their feet seeming not to touch the floor.

But the most entertaining of the dancers was
Dr. Jean Roy, who had arrived late and by herself.
But wait, she did have a partner! It was a life-
size mannequin made from cloth with a photo
face pasted onto a large ball for a head. On its
head was a gentleman's top hat, and the feet
were fastened to the top of Dr. Roy's shoes, so
that they moved in perfectly synchronous steps.
She held his left arm out stiffly with her right one
and swooped around the floor in exact time to
the music, a comic parody of the Soliers. As she
danced closer to their vantage point, Christina
could see a sign on his back identifying him. Mis-
ter Darcy, of course!

The dancing paused as the revelers lined up for the buffet supper. James, scanning the crowd below said, "Where are Cecil and Thorpe? They were here earlier. I'm suspecting they are up to no good." He excused himself, telling Christina to wait for him to help her down the ladder, and he hurried down to check with his father and Tommy.

It seemed ages, and Christina was getting hungry. She feared being too embarrassed to be caught hiding in the loft, so she kept back from view. When James finally returned with apologies for being gone so long, he explained, "We are rid of Cecil and Thorpe. They were trying to burglarize the house! I'll tell you all about it later. Let's go down and join the party."

As the diners were enjoying the sumptuous supper, the distant storm had come closer. The wind rattled the upper hay hatches and blew through the cracks, causing the candle lanterns to flicker. As a loud roar came down, Tommy yelled, "Hailstorm!" and ran out the door toward the meadow. "Hotshot!" he called. "Come here, Boy!" And the horse, already running wildly, came toward him, the hailstones falling like missiles around him. Tommy threw open the big wagon door, admitting a deluge of water and ice. The horse stepped onto the dance floor, steaming and tossing his head wildly. The crowd drew back in amazement, and as Tommy tried to calm him, the lights went out, leaving only the little candle lanterns flickering along the buffet and on the tables.

Tommy continued talking to calm Hotshot. Mr. Chamber, director of the Queen's Chamber musicians, summoned his players and lifted his baton for them to play softly "Minuet in G." The slow rhythmic melody seemed to have an effect on the crazed animal, and Tommy sent for salve to doctor a few bloody spots where the huge hailstones had cut into Hotshot's shoulders.

In a few minutes the power was restored and the lights came back on. Some of the children crowded around wanting to pet the horse and offer carrots from the relish trays, but Tommy told them to stand back because Hotshot was injured and wouldn't understand their kind gestures.

The storm stopped more quickly than it had begun, the water was mopped from the dance floor, and the men went outside to see to their cars, some of which now sported big dimples and dents from the falling ice. They came back bringing Ping-Pong size hailstones to show the partyers.

Christina's family stood in amazement. Mr. Dashwood exclaimed, "Tina, you were right. This is wild country. Everything is bigger than normal, even the weather."

The dancing resumed and Tommy led Hotshot back to his stable. Then a huge birthday cake was wheeled in on a cart and Jane blew out her candles while the crowd sang first, "Happy Birthday," then the Spanish "Las Mañanitas." The band struck up a ranchero tune for a quick dance before several of the diners assembled to watch Jane open the huge pile of gifts.

Most did not notice that at the back of the hall the Fairfax men and Mr. Dashwood had unobtrusively formed a little knot around Monsieur Solier. Like a troop of soldiers escorting a prisoner, they edged him toward the rear door, and out into the dark. After a long interval they returned and dispersed quietly, but a few people noticed that Monsieur Solier had turned very pale, and that his hands trembled as he picked up his coffee cup.

No one ever knew what had transpired. Some who had noticed the group's departure thought they had gone outside to smoke. One man surmised that Solier had groped another man's wife and the men had "taken him to the woodshed." We will never know whether the men threatened him or reprimanded him physically. But for our private information, be it known that Monsieur

Solier never, ever, from that moment on, mistreated his wife again.

The party lasted long past midnight. The older folks had already departed, and the younger ones with their importunate insistence kept the musicians going to the point of exhaustion. Finally, they played, "Home Sweet Home," letting everyone know it was their last dance.

Some couples were lingering in the shadows, the helpers were beginning to clear away the remains of the banquet, and Mrs. Fairfax ordered the ladder to the hayloft taken down to prevent any smooching upstairs.

James and Christina had enjoyed the last waltz together, and now still stood facing each other. "You're leaving with your folks tomorrow?" he asked. "Will you write to me?"

"Yes, it would be fun to correspond with you."

"Has Tommy asked you to write to him?"

"Tommy hasn't asked me to write, but he knows I'll be corresponding with Jane. And I want to hear news of the family."

"I think Tommy is planning to ride back with your family as far as La Junta in order to show you Bent's Fort. Do you mind if I come along?"

"Oh, I hope you can! Please do. Is Jane coming too?"

"I think she and her new real dad want more time to go over Phyllida's diaries together." He moved closer and took her hand.

She held her breath. But he, not sure if her acquiescence was mere politeness or a special regard for himself, merely squeezed her hand, gently released it, and said, "I'll walk you to the house."

Chapter XXXI

It was a delightful visit—perfect, in
being much too short.

—Jane Austen

The next morning Christina was honored at a surprise breakfast. As she entered the dining room, everyone rose and applauded. There was a huge banner with balloons across the wall and the letters THANK YOU TINA. Astounded, she asked the reason.

"My father and I want to thank you for bringing us together," said Jane. "It was due to you that we found each other. And we want you to have this gift as a token of our gratitude." She handed Christina a box containing a silver charm bracelet. Each if the six charms was a tiny book

labeled with the name of one of Jane Austen's
books. Christina thanked them, and declared the
gift to be most appropriate because it was Jane
Austen, she said, who really deserved the credit.
"And also, Mr. Saxon," she added, "because he
is the one who brought Jane Austen to Tondaga
High School." She hugged her thanks to Jane for
the bracelet and for the invitation to return the
following summer.

As the goodbyes were being said, a phone call
changed the plans for travel. James was being
requested by a dean from the University in Albuquerque for a special interview the following
day and would be unable to accompany them to
Bent's Fort.

Christina's heart sank. Tommy would be an
entertaining tour guide, but she preferred having the company of James for one more day. His
look as he shook her hand during the goodbyes
made her think that he also regretted the change
in plans.

After the goodbyes, including tearful hugs between Jane and Christina, the station wagon with
suitcases on top started down the winding road
toward Santa Fe and Lamy.

But back at the ranch another change oc-
curred. After a phone call to the University,
James sat at the kitchen table and wrote a brief

message. Taking it to his father's office, he asked Mr. Fairfax for a special favor.

"Dad, I'm afraid you won't approve, but as a favor to me, will you sign this with your name?"

Edward Fairfax pushed aside his account books, took the paper and began to laugh. "So Tommy's up to his old tricks, is he? I see it's going to be a battle between brothers for the hand of the fair Christina. Well, I'll say my complicity in this scheme is excused by the old saying 'All's fair in love and war'." And he signed the paper with a chuckle and went back to his accounts.

Due to the extended goodbyes and the last minute call for James, Tommy worried that they'd be late to the train and he drove faster than usual, keeping a lookout for police patrols. They arrived at Lamy station without incident and with just enough time for checking their bags. While they were doing so, Lilly became acquainted with a red-haired girl of about her own age who was holding a beagle puppy. "What a cute dog! Are you taking him on the train?"

"No, I can't. I just got him, but I'm going to visit my grandmother in Kansas City before school starts, so I have to leave him at home. My parents got him for me for my birthday. They'll take care of him till I get back next week. I'm by myself.

Will you sit with me on the train?" Her father took the puppy and looked approvingly at Lilly.

"Yes. I have some Lexicon cards and we can play games in the observation car. My sister will be sitting with her boyfriend."

They heard the whistle and looked up to see the red and silver engine coming around the bend. The train was about ten minutes late, so as soon as the passengers were boarded, the train moved away from the station. After the conductor had taken their tickets, Lilly went to the observation car to find her new friend. Tommy sat with Christina and proved to be as expert a tour guide as Jane had been, telling interesting stories about the Santa Fe Trail. He was especially enthusiastic about Bent's Fort.

"DuVon Films will be doing a movie here this fall. I've already applied to be an extra. If you'd been here last month, I'd have gotten you in. I know the director. You don't need to worry about your chipped tooth because Pierre would put you in a crowd scene, but you do have to wear authentic old-time clothes. It's going to be a documentary."

"Will you have a big part?"

"I'll be in one of the close-up scenes where the scouts ride up ahead of a wagon. Pierre knows I'm a good rider, and I'll have Hotshot here."

"Will Jane be in the film too?"

"She didn't sign up because it's her week to start college, and she didn't want to miss classes. If it was only high school, she would probably be here in a lot of scenes. They usually have tutors on set for younger kids who are missing school. Pat and Ed Blazer, the people we'll be staying with tonight, are retired teachers who usually tutor movie kids."

After about half an hour the conductor returned. "Are you Thomas Fairfax? This message came for you." Tommy opened it and found a telegram from his father.

EMERGENCY AT HOME. YOU ARE NEEDED HERE. JAMES WILL PICK YOU UP AT LAS VEGAS. DAD

"Damn!" muttered Tommy. "I wonder what happened." He gathered up his bag and camera and after a quick good bye went to the end of the car to exit. As the train slowed, he saw James waiting close to the tracks. As Tommy stepped down, James slid past him and boarded the train.

"What's going on? What happened?" Tommy asked.

"Hotshot!"

"What's wrong?"

"You'll find out."

"Aren't you coming?" The train began to pull away.

"I'm not needed. I'll take your seat. No use wasting a good ticket." James tossed the car keys for Tommy to catch, and smiled at seeing Tommy left on the platform with a stupefied look on his face.

James found Christina and took the seat next to her, laughing in triumph, as he explained what had happened. The call for James' interview in Albuquerque had proved to be a hoax. Because James had called the University immediately and found out that Tommy had tricked him in order to keep him home, he had prevailed on his father to reverse the trick by sending the telegram. There was no emergency at the ranch. James had won the battle of the brothers for the seat next to Christina on the trip to Bent's Fort!

Christina was flattered to be the focus of attention, and especially gratified that it was James who had prevailed. Their laughing conversation was interrupted by the attendant's asking if they wanted reservations for dinner in the dining car.

They went forward to find Lilly, who chose to eat in the snack bar with her new friend. So James and Christina joined her parents at a table for four, and as they enjoyed their meal, James explained the change in traveling companions.

"I'll be your guide to Bent's Fort. I'm sure Tommy would want me to explain the history, and I'll do so with Pat and Ed's help."

"I hope there's nothing too seriously wrong at the ranch," said Mrs. Dashwood.

"I'll call from the Fort," said James. "Where animals are concerned, more help is always needed." He quickly turned the conversation back to the party, and Mr. Dashwood made another change of subject by asking more details about how William Saxon had found his daughter.

After James and Christina reviewed the incidents that had led up to the discovery, Mrs. Dashwood asked about the sudden departure of the men from the dance floor. "John left me standing in the middle of a two-step, and never told me what it was all about."

Mr. Dashwood apologized and said, "Well, we decided that in order to protect the people involved, we would tell no one what transpired."

James added, "You can say he was initiated into the Secret Society of Barns and Buffoons."

After they laughed, Mr. Dashwood said, "Without revealing exactly how the meeting was conducted in the stable that night, I want to say that you, Young Man, are a gifted speaker. Your powers of persuasion without threats, your calm delivery and choice of words were excellent. With that silver tongue, you should be a candidate for public office or for the pulpit."

James accepted his compliments graciously and turned the credit back to Christina for detecting the bad situation in the first place. "And Christina's remembering the ring and Mr. Saxon's hand was the catalyst for the grand reunion for my sister."

"But tell about the second group departure," said Christina. "How did you know that Cecil and Thorpe were in the house?"

"José was the one who alerted us. He had gone out to check the horses, and on the way back noticed that the light at the back door of the house went off suddenly. He decided to investigate and noticed that their big black car was parked at the front door. He saw flashes of light in the windows as if someone was inside with a flashlight."

"Then he ran back to get you from the dance, but how did he manage to round up all you Fairfax men without alarming the whole crowd of us?"

"Probably with a secret handshake of the Barn Buffoons," laughed Christina.

"We divided up, with some watching the front door, where they had planned to escape, and Dad with his rifle going in the back door. He flipped

the light switch on for the main part of the house
and there they were!"

"Had they already taken some things?" asked
Christina.

"Caught red-handed with a suitcase open on
the coffee table, filled with turquoise necklaces,
rings, concho belt, and even some black pottery.
Dad held them at gunpoint while José searched
their car and their cabin. Tommy and I went
through their pockets, and looked in the other
rooms to check for anything missing."

"When did the police come?"

"They didn't. Dad said, 'We're calling the police
as soon as you are on the road. You need to get
out of New Mexico, and I'd suggest out of the
country. There will be an all-points-bulletin out
for you, with names and descriptions, so you better get across the Colorado border mighty fast.'
He never did call the police, but they didn't know
that, and I think we're rid of them for good."

At La Junta they were met by Pat and Ed
Blazer, an attractive and personable couple, Tommy and James' Santa Fe Trail friends, who drove
them to the Fort.

Bent's Fort was a huge adobe reconstruction
of the original trading post built in the 1800's. It
was the only place between Independence and
Santa Fe where travelers on the Santa Fe Trail

could rest and replenish their supplies. Docents clothed in frontier garb toured them through the rooms, and explained about daily life at the Fort in the 1800's. Pat and Ed added more details.

"What's that machine with the big screw in the patio?" asked Christina.

"That's a press for the buffalo hides," Ed explained. "The dried hides would be easier to ship back east. Beaver pelts didn't take up so much room, but the beaver trade did not last."

"Why not?"

"The tall beaver hats went out of fashion in Europe and in our country," said Pat. "But I like to think of this place as a peaceful oasis, and for a short time an example of friendship between races. It was one of the few times in history that the Cheyenne, Arapaho, Kiowa, and other tribes camped together and were admitted inside the Fort to trade."

"Why didn't it last?"

"Too many settlers, too few buffalo, no more wood for wagon repair, polluted water holes, and tension between Indians and whites."

"Plus the cholera epidemic," added Ed. "Then the U.S. Army used the Fort as a headquarters for the war against Mexico, but would not purchase the Fort from the Bents."

Our tourists found a little shop replicating one where the early Indians would trade furs for trinkets and necessary items. After the tour they browsed through it and then through the bookshop where they purchased reading material for the long train ride home. Lilly bought the picture book *Without a Wagon,* telling of five women who had hiked the entire Santa Fe Trail. Mr. Dashwood bought *Perilous Pursuit on the Santa Fe Trail.* Mrs. Dashwood chose *Persuaded: A Great Lakes Story* because Christina said it was based on one of Jane Austen's books. James did not reveal his purchase until they were outside. Instead of walking with the others back toward the parking area, he led Christina along a path by the Arkansas River in back of the Fort.

Seeing Lilly wading in the river, James said, "Let's cool our feet," and began taking off his shoes. Christina agreed and as they stepped into the water, he took her hand as if to steady her, but held it toward him and slid a tiny bone ring on her little finger, saying, "Here's your souvenir, Christina. This will help you remember the Southwest, and it can be a reminder for you to write to me."

"I won't need to be reminded. I love it," she replied. "It just fits. How perfect!"

"I'm hoping it can be more than a reminder ring. Do you think it could be called a promise ring?" He brought her hand up to his cheek. "Do you think it could serve as a promise to give you a better one? One that fits on your third finger?" He leaned closer.

She turned her face up to him, and whispered, "Yes."

The picture of the two lovers standing in the water, their tentative embrace with the ripples lapping at their ankles would delight any artist or a writer hoping to prolong this scene, but the romantic moment was cut short by Lilly's call from the corner of the fort where she had run with shoes and stockings in hand to respond to her mother's beckoning. "Hurry up!" Lilly called. "We're leaving!" Their tête-à-tête interrupted, the couple walked hand in hand to join the others.

****

Christina's heart sang with the motion of the train all the way back to Michigan. Lilly declared, "Tina, you're not only a heroine, but you're engaged too!"

Christina denied the engaged part, but who can doubt that, in time, it would be so. She had indeed found her real hero. The only doubt later, upon James' applying to her parents for the permission to seal their promise to each other, was Mrs. Dashwood's concern about the discrepancy in their ages.

"Don't you think," she asked her husband, "that James is a little too old for Christina?"

But Mr. Dashwood reminded her of the greater difference between their own ages, saying, "And our marriage has shown the test of time rather well, don't you think? And I believe that neither I nor James is ready to wear a flannel waistcoat."

The reader can assume, as the compression of these pages must show, that the end of our tale is near, resulting in almost complete felicity for all. But the rules of composition declare that no loose ends shall remain.

The noises on the third floor of Buttery Cottage were never explained to anyone's satisfaction, so we must leave it to the reader to determine whether there was a real ghost, or merely a sound caused by the branches of the big cottonwood tree knocking against the attic roof.

And what about Tommy and Jane? Realizing that they were not blood relation, had been best buddies since childhood, and had met no other persons to capture their hearts, they eventually married.

And Mr. Saxon? He moved to Santa Fe to be near them and in time, to learn the joys of being a grandfather.

Finis

About the Author

Inez Ross lived on a farm in Michigan, attended Michigan State University, lived with her forester husband in Wyoming, and moved to New Mexico where she taught high school English. Her hobbies, in addition to reading Jane Austen, are jogging, stargazing, and hiking on the Santa Fe Trail. She has one daughter and a granddaughter, to whom this book is dedicated.

About Jane Austen

Jane Austen is the greatest novelist in English. Born in 1775 in Hampshire, England, she grew up in a large family of boys with only one sister, who became her favorite companion. Except for a short stay at a boarding school, she was educated at home by reading under the encouragement of her clergyman father. She began writing at an early age and took part in family theatricals.

Aside from her early writing and a few unfinished works, she is remembered mostly for her six novels: *Pride and Prejudice*, *Northanger Abbey*, *Sense and Sensibility*, *Emma*, *Mansfield Park*, and *Persuasion*.

She is known for her realistic portrayal of human relationships, her humor, elegantly understated style, and her satire of bourgeois snobbery and hypocrisy. She died in England in 1817.

A favorite short biography is *Jane Austen* by Carol Shields. A useful and entertaining reference is *Jane Austen for Dummies* by Joan Klingel Ray.

About JASNA

The Jane Austen Society of North America is an organization dedicated to the enjoyment and appreciation of Jane Austen and her writing. There are approximately 4,000 members and over 60 regional groups in the U.S. and Canada. JASNA was founded in New York in 1979.

Each autumn several hundred members gather for the Annual General Meeting (AGM) at a city in the U.S. or Canada for a three-day conference with lectures by scholars and members, entertainments, tours, exhibits, and workshops. (You may choose Regency dance lessons, or bonnet making, for example.) The AGM culminates in a banquet and Regency ball. Many attend in costume. At a recent AGM, costumed members paraded down a Chicago street before the ball.

JASNA News is mailed to members three times a year. The journals *Persuasions* and *Persuasions On-line* are published annually. The society also conducts an annual student Essay Contest and sponsors occasional tours to England. You can learn about joining a chapter, find the location of the next AGM, read comments on Austen films, or find merchandise for sale by visiting the website at http://www.jasna.org